COLOMBIAN
GOLD

COLOMBIAN GOLD

A NOVEL OF POWER AND CORRUPTION

JAIME MANRIQUE

TRANSLATION BY SARA NELSON AND JAIME MANRIQUE

Clarkson N. Potter, Inc./Publishers

DISTRIBUTED BY CROWN PUBLISHERS, INC.   NEW YORK

This is a work of fiction. The characters, incidents, places, dialogues and speeches are products of the author's imagination and are not to be construed as real. The author's use of names of actual persons, living or dead, is incidental to the purposes of the plot and is not intended to change the entirely fictional character of the work.

Copyright © 1983 by Jaime Manrique

Published by Clarkson N. Potter, Inc.
One Park Avenue, New York, New York 10016 and simultaneously in Canada by General Publishing Company Limited.

Manufactured in the United States of America

Library of Congress Cataloging in Publication Data

Manrique, Jaime.
  Colombian gold.
  I. Title.
PQ8180.23.A52C6   1983   863   83-3978
ISBN 0-517-546493

Designed by Beth Tondreau

10 9 8 7 6 5 4 3 2 1
First Edition

FOR BILL SULLIVAN, MIGUEL FALQUEZ,
AND RAY SAWHILL

ACKNOWLEDGMENTS

I would like to thank my editor, Carol Southern, and my agent, Thomas Colchie, for their enthusiasm, and Sarah Arvio and Martha Cummings for their help with the manuscript. I would also like to express my deepest appreciation to the following people for their support: Eugenie Nable, Margaret Finnegan, Dan Wilson, Raphael Mostel, Tomar Levine, Ben Ami Fihman, Vicente Ching, and Helen O'Donnell.

I
CARNIVAL

Our lives are the rivers
that flow into the sea
of death;
Great lords go there
to die
and be consumed;
There, the great rivers,
the brooks
and the streams,
Are the same
for those who live by their hands
and those by their wealth.

JORGE MANRIQUE
*"Couplets on the Death of His
Father,"
ca. 1475*

1 ▽

The telephone rang in the bedroom. Santiago thought about unplugging it but realized the call might be important. He opened his eyes. It was dawn.

Santiago knew the ringing had not wakened his wife, who never rose before noon. The house could collapse and Beatrice would continue her deep Valium sleep. Despite his own drowsiness, he was aware that it was the last day of carnival, that he was at his father's house in Barranquilla, and that his father lay gravely ill in the hospital.

He lifted the receiver.

"Hello, may I speak to Santiago Villalba?" said an urgent voice at the other end of the line.

"Speaking," he mumbled.

"Santiago, this is Dr. Martínez. I'm sorry to waken you but I'm afraid I have bad news. Your father has taken a turn for the worse." There was a pause. "I believe he wants to talk to you. He has been calling your name."

"Thank you, doctor. I'm on my way," he said. Beatrice, her face buried under a pillow, hadn't stirred; he'd never understood how she could sleep like that without smothering herself. Her long blond curls fanned out across her shoulders. He decided to let her sleep; after a hurried arrival in Barranquilla from Miami, they had gone to bed well past midnight.

He got up and lit a cigarette. He was in no hurry to get to the hospital. Looking around, he realized that he'd never been in the room before. He had, in fact, only visited his father's house once, and on that occasion he'd been received in the living room. Now, through the window, he could see the interior garden, its yellow, red, and white cannonballs, orange and pink hibiscus, and scarlet bougainvillea in full bloom. A bird sang; it reminded him of a *turpial* he had had as a child. Its cage had hung outside his bedroom window, and every morning he would awaken to its melody. This bird, twittering and chirping, was probably a small one. Its song was shy and melancholy.

Opening the window, Santiago leaned on the sill, his eyes wandering beyond the house and across the red clay roofs to the flowering acacias on the street. A mild breeze blew a salty aroma through the shrubs and trees. He put his cigarette out, went into the bathroom, and stood under the shower for a few minutes. As he toweled briskly, he caught himself whistling. He dressed in jeans, loafers, and a blue Oxford shirt. After dabbing on cologne, he sat at the desk and wrote Beatrice a note: "Darling, I'll be at the hospital. Call you at noon."

It was growing light. The bird had stopped singing; the flowers gave off an intoxicating scent. Santiago walked downstairs. In his childhood, he had often fantasized about the inside of this house. He made his way through several rooms, noting the high ceilings and elaborate Arabian tiles. Exuberant tropical plants grew in huge tubs, and paintings decorated the walls: sunsets, dawn over the waves, fishermen casting their nets, sailboats, sharks and swordfish, coral, iridescent seashells. And the furniture was lavish: Art Deco tables and chairs, French chaises in faded pink and yellow velvet, enormous mirrors with heavy gilt frames, wicker rocking chairs, solid mahogany chests.

In the music room was a Steinway grand, and in the library were black walnut bookcases lined with volumes bound in dark leather. Santiago leafed through several books that lay open and discovered that his father had been spending his old age reading Teilhard de Chardin; the margins were full of notes in Alvaro Villalba's shaky handwriting. Oil paintings of Santiago's ancestors hung on the library walls: the dukes and counts and marquises who in fifteenth-century Spain had fought for the unification of the empire; the viceroy Villalba who had come to America in the seventeenth century with a coffin in which he slept to remind him of his mortality. There were portraits and busts of relatives who had been heroes and heroines of Colombian independence, and sepia photographs of his grandfather, General Villalba Uribe, whom he had never met, and of his grandmother, serene and distant. More recent photographs were scattered throughout the room, too, including one of his father's wife—his stepmother. He stood for a while in front of a picture of his half-sister, who had died of cancer. Santiago had met her only once, one afternoon when she had come to visit him at boarding school. She was smiling in the photograph, taken before illness wasted her.

He didn't know if it was the early hour or that he was alone and making the tour of this sprawling mansion for the first time, but he found something chilling about the place.

In the garage he saw Pedro asleep on a stool, his head leaning against the wall. His father's chauffeur for years, Pedro was not yet fifty but seemed much older. Santiago moved quietly, but when he turned the door handle Pedro jerked awake.

"Señor Villalba." He was embarrassed, as if sleeping were a sin. "Do you want me to drive you somewhere?"

Santiago loved to ride through empty city streets early in the morning. He decided he would rather drive alone. "Thank you, Pedro. It's all right. Go back to sleep. I'm going to the hospital to see my father."

"Give my regards to Don Alvaro," Pedro called as Santiago started the car. "Tell him I've been praying for him."

He backed out slowly. The sky was still dark blue and a wind raced through the tops of the blossoming pink *matarratones*. A flock of pelicans, wheeling back and forth, sketched a V in the sky. Except for an occasional drunkard and a few cars full of raucous people still carrying on last night's party, the streets were deserted.

He parked but did not get out immediately. He turned on the radio to carnival music. The lines of a song he had learned in childhood came back to him: *Este es el amor, amor,/el amor que me divierte/cuando estoy en la parranda/no me acuerdo de la muerte*. He switched the radio off and made his way to the entrance. As he pushed open the hospital door, a medicinal smell surrounded him. It was almost day and all the lights were on, but the building seemed empty. It's as though the patients are out celebrating carnival, as though death is on a holiday, he thought.

A receptionist stood up behind the counter. "Good morning. Don Santiago?" she asked. "Dr. Martínez is expecting you. Room 206."

The hospital had once been a private mansion. A turquoise carpet snaked down the middle of the marble staircase and muffled the sound of his steps.

The second-floor corridor was white and brightly lit. He knocked on the door of his father's room; a nurse opened it. Dr. Martínez, a gray-haired man almost his father's age, was sitting by Alvaro Villalba's bedside.

"Ah, I'm very glad you're here," the doctor said. He extended his hand.

His formality made Santiago uneasy. Wasn't the impending death of an old man the most natural thing in the world? "Is it very serious?" he asked, shaking Martínez's knobby hand.

"Yes. But he might last a few more days—it's hard to say exactly. I'm not sure how much longer his heart can take the strain. He's gone back to sleep now."

The three of them gazed solemnly at the old man. Finally, Santiago told the doctor and nurse to get some rest, that he wanted to be alone with his father for a while. If anything happened, he would call for help.

Alone now, Santiago stared at his father. A plastic tube was taped to his left arm, and his mouth was agape. A whitish beard blurred his cheeks and jowls. He was more than eighty years old, and he had been dying for the last twenty of them. Just the year before he had tried a hormone treatment in Rumania.

For a long time Santiago had loathed this man. When his mother died, Santiago's hatred for him was so great it obscured the pain he felt at his mother's loss; Santiago put the blame for her death on his father. Now, he thought, pouring himself a glass of water, he could look at his father dispassionately, as little more than a fountain from which a great fortune would spring. A rush of memories enveloped him as he sat beside the unconscious old man.

Santiago's mother, Isadora, had been born into a family at a time when their roller-coaster fortune was on the descent. By the time she was fifteen she had become a great beauty, and suitors were offering acres of land and heads of cattle for her hand. At sixteen, her parents married her to a local rancher who was forty years older than she. There was a child who died in infancy.

One day a Bogotá aristocrat with a penchant for cock-fighting appeared in town. Alvaro Villalba was already more than fifty but still dashing. Isadora fell in love with him, left her husband, broke with her parents, and became his mistress. He settled his beautiful young lover on a banana plantation. When she gave birth to Santiago, Villalba moved mother and child to the seaport of Barranquilla, so Isadora could bring the boy up in a less-isolated environment.

Santiago spent much of his first seven years on the Caribbean beaches, seeing his father on weekends, and when Villalba was in the city on business. Saturday mornings Santiago's nanny would take him to his parents' bedroom. Alvaro Villalba, who scorned the black and Indian blood that flowed in Isadora's family's veins, would give Santiago a hundred pesos if he recited correctly the surnames of his Spanish ancestors: Villalba, Santamaría, Herrera, Suarez, Casanueva, Uribe, Villalba Folgoso, Alvarez, Arias, Benitez, Salazar y Pizarro y Villalba. After a successful quiz, Villalba would exclaim, "A true blueblood!"

One night Villalba surprised Isadora dancing in a club with her young lover. He had a second mistress himself, but couldn't abide Isadora's flaunting her affair in public, and used the incident as an excuse to separate.

Cut off from both Villalba and her husband, too proud to go to her parents for help, Isadora was destitute. She took Santiago and moved to Bogotá, renting an airless room in the center of town, where she survived for a while by pawning the emeralds and diamonds and pearls and finally the clothes that Villalba had given her. Wan but still beautiful, she began bringing men back to the room, leaving Santiago in the care of the concierge. She ate little. Within a few months she began to show the first symptoms of tuberculosis.

During her last days, Isadora, bedridden, spent the long nights coughing and spitting blood, while Santiago, terrified, watched her strength seep away.

Then an item appeared in the newspaper indicating that Alvaro Villalba was in Bogotá on business. Isadora dragged herself out of bed, washed, and dressed in her best clothes. That evening, avoiding the concierge, she took Santiago and walked across the city in the rain to Villalba's.

The butler led the mother and child into the kitchen, where they drank hot chocolate and ate bread and cheese. Eventually, the butler announced that Alvaro

Villalba would receive them in the library. They found Don Alvaro sitting by the fireplace reading a newspaper.

Greeting them politely, he indicated that they should sit down. Isadora, explaining that she was ill, asked him to assume responsibility for their son. Villalba cut her off and reminded her that he already had a daughter; that it wasn't proper to take a "love child" in to live with his legitimate family. But he offered to give Isadora money for doctors and help for the boy. After writing out a check, he hugged the boy and whispered, "You'll always be a Villalba." Then he stood up to signal the end of the meeting and walked out of the room.

The butler showed them out the front door.

Three days later, Isadora died.

Villalba, who now had no choice but to recognize the boy legally, saw to the burial plans and arranged to send the child to study at an exclusive Bogotá academy. Each Christmas he received his son. In these "interviews," conducted in his Santa Marta office, Villalba would ask Santiago about school, give him a check in return for a quick kiss on the cheek, and bid him goodbye until the next year.

During his school years, Santiago made one friend— Mario Simán, whose father was the Minister of Foreign Relations. Mario had lost his left leg in a terrorist attack, and although the other students did not openly ridicule him, they shunned him, regarding him as a freak. Santiago sought out Mario's friendship.

Through Mario, whose parents often invited him to spend weekends at their home in Bogotá or at their country house, Santiago began to see a little of the world. Yet his feelings of loneliness and isolation were not assuaged. He was subject to frequent spells of melancholy, and together with Mario, he plotted to stage a suicide. He would throw himself off the roof of the school building, break a few bones, attract his father's attention, and make the old man regret his past neglect. Villalba would, Santiago hoped, beg for forgiveness, take him to live in the big house, and give him the love Santiago imagined other parents bestowed on their children.

When it came time to jump, he lost his nerve. Mario gave him a helpful but ill-timed push, and instead of falling in the garden Santiago landed in a cypress tree, fracturing two vertebrae and both arms and legs. He was confined to bed for months. Mario visited him every day, bringing books, candy, and puzzles, but Santiago waited in vain for a visit from his father. Time passed. A few gifts arrived, their cards signed by Nury, his father's secretary.

Alvaro Villalba arrived one gray afternoon at the end of the school year, bringing a wrapped package that Santiago hoped was a box of chocolates. Tearing through the silver paper, Santiago found a book called *The Tragic Sense of Life*.

Villalba told Santiago that since the teachers at the school thought he needed special attention, he had decided to send him to a small boarding school in the United States, where the instructors might be better able to help him. Santiago, although stunned, understood that he was being sent to a place where he would be out of his father's way. It would, he feared, be a kind of exile from which there would be no return.

Don Alvaro half-opened his eyes and looked at his visitor. In his delirium he might not know who I am, thought

Santiago. The old man's dry, cracked lips began to open, as if he were trying to speak, and Santiago had a moment of terror: Don Alvaro wasn't going to die after all. He would improve in a few days, and soon they'd transfer him to a hospital in the United States, where they'd cure him as they had so many times before. He would come back to Colombia perfectly well, and his life would linger on for years, years during which he would want to see Santiago, would expect him to visit, would want him to run his affairs, and—worse—would demand attention and care, everything that he himself had denied his son.

The old man's hands began moving over the sheet. Santiago shrank back in horror, and thought bitterly of the many times in his childhood when he had craved contact with these hands, the many times he had longed to hear kind words.

Villalba choked out a few unintelligible sounds. Santiago felt fury rise up inside him; he didn't want to hear what his father had to say. He wanted to see him die. For a moment, his conscience stung with the realization that he felt not a trace of compassion.

Suddenly he snatched up the pillow and placed it firmly over his father's face. He held it there, pushing down with all his strength. The old man's hands fluttered, the left one grasping for Santiago's elbow, and his body contracted in a last burst of strength.

Santiago removed the pillow and let out a long sigh. His father's face was red, the eyelids open, the eyes glazed. With trembling, sweaty fingers, he closed the eyelids, replaced the pillow, and rearranged the sheet.

Alvaro Villalba looked like the same man he had been

a few minutes before, except that he had stopped breathing. Now he was dead.

Santiago lit a cigarette and began to count to a hundred. A creamy, gluey liquid ran down one leg; he had ejaculated.

Breathless, he went into the bathroom and turned on the hot water. Lowering his pants, he wiped himself with moistened toilet paper. After cleaning himself carefully, he returned to the room.

He lit another cigarette and counted to ten. To avoid looking at the corpse, he closed his eyes.

Minutes later, he peered into the corridor. No one was there, but the hospital was stirring; noises came from other rooms.

Santiago returned to the bedside and dialed the receptionist. "This is room 206. I fell asleep for a minute, and when I woke up, I found my father de—de—" His voice broke and he began to weep convulsively.

"Un momento, por favor," the woman said. "Calm down. Calm down."

The attack intensified. He was still weeping when the nurse arrived on the run, and it was through sobs that he refused Dr. Martínez's offer of a sedative and a ride home.

When he left the hospital, his eyes were still blinded by tears. In the stark sunlight, the street was filling up with people, but Santiago went on weeping.

2

He drove aimlessly until the sobbing stopped. In the barrios, salsa music blasted from dance halls and cantinas, and laughing, screeching people in ghost costumes and wildly patterned *capuchones* raced by. Relief, then pleasure, surged through Santiago. For the first time, he felt free.

As he drove into the quiet, shady neighborhood where the Villalba home was situated, the din of the barrios still rang in his ears. Any festivities in this part of town are going on behind closed doors, he thought.

It was when he parked in front of the house that the realization of the change in his fortunes overwhelmed him. He was sole son and heir. His sister was dead. His stepmother too. In Colombia an estate cannot be diverted from the children of the deceased; bastard or not, this was his property. From now on, he was master of the Villalba fortune.

Nury opened the front door. "I'm sorry about your

father, Don Santiago," she said, holding out her hand and smiling weakly. "The telephone's been ringing off the hook all morning. I finally unplugged the one on the second floor so that Doña Beatriz wouldn't be disturbed." She paused. "You don't know how much I loved him."

Santiago touched her hand and walked by. He tried to imagine the kind of love this woman could have felt for Villalba, who would have scorned her as he scorned everyone he considered his inferior.

It wasn't yet noon. Santiago went to the bar, poured himself a double scotch, and gazed out into the garden. The liquor pricked his tongue.

In the early 1970s, after Santiago had finished boarding school in Connecticut, his father had insisted he move to Washington and study diplomacy at Georgetown University. There, again at Villalba's insistence, he introduced himself to Alfredo Fernández, a business partner of his father's who had just been made Colombian ambassador to the United States. It wasn't long before Santiago heard rumors: Fernández, aware that the bottom would soon drop out of Colombia's banana trade, was supposed to have taken personal charge of the Colombia–U.S. marijuana traffic.

Fernández took Santiago under his wing, and it was at an embassy dinner party that Santiago, only a few months away from graduation, met the ambassador's granddaughter, Beatrice.

A cousin of Beatrice's had told Santiago about the girl. She had just arrived from New York, where she had been hospitalized; she had studied in Switzerland and at the Sorbonne; she was beautiful, and she was a good marriage prospect.

That spring night, as he wandered through the garden paths, Santiago approached Beatrice, who was sitting alone on a bench under a cherry tree. When he sat beside her, he noticed that her face, despite its beauty, looked neither fresh nor young; her skin was drawn and tight, as if made of plastic.

They talked for hours that night and began to see each other regularly. In July they announced their engagement; in October they married. The Fernández family was very pleased. Villalba wrote his son a long congratulatory letter, the first time he had made such a gesture.

What Santiago hadn't been told and learned only much later was that Beatrice was a family headache. It was whispered that her father, the ambassador's eldest son, had offered a million dollars to the person who would take the girl off his hands.

While still a student at the Sorbonne, Beatrice had fallen in love with an Italian count, who had died in a car accident. Beatrice suffered a nervous breakdown and her doctors had her confined in a Swiss sanitarium. There she slit her wrists and slashed her face with a piece of glass.

Over the next two years, Beatrice attempted suicide repeatedly. Transferred to a mental hospital outside New York City, she refused food and had to be fed intravenously. She was given plastic surgery and extensive psychiatric help. At first her parents visited her frequently, but soon they gave up; her situation had become an embarrassment. Then a New York doctor discovered a tumor in her brain. It was removed, and Beatrice seemed to improve.

When Santiago met her, she was recovering from further surgery on her face and could not go out in daylight or use makeup. Still, he was extremely attracted to her. He understood later that her suffering was for him an aphrodisiac. He identified with her because she was a victim and so was he.

He'd hoped to become an academic, but his father and in-laws, delighted with the marriage, had other plans. They had him slated for a job in Colombian politics. The ambassador found him a position as an attaché at the embassy in Madrid. It was assumed that after a short time, Santiago would return home to run for office. Santiago felt that he had finally begun a reconciliation with his father, and with the world.

They enjoyed the first months in Madrid. Santiago was enthusiastic about his job, and the couple had time to travel around Spain. Then Beatrice became pregnant —much to her family's relief and happiness. Villalba himself, eager for the birth of a grandchild, made a special trip to Madrid.

When Beatrice was in her tenth week, Santiago received a call from the maid. It was an emergency, she said. He should come home immediately.

Everything happened in a blur. An hour later, Beatrice was lying in shock in the emergency room. The miscarried baby had been a boy. The doctors said there was no reason why Beatrice could not have another child, but she became extremely depressed. Nothing and no one could cheer her up. Her parents came; after a few weeks they saw they were helpless and returned home.

Thinking a change of scene would help, Santiago accepted an offer from Fernández to work in Tampa, Florida. Santiago's father bought them a house on the Gulf. The Florida climate agreed with Beatrice; she seemed less depressed and looked forward to another pregnancy.

But Santiago grew increasingly disillusioned with his work. It became clear to him why his father-in-law had chosen him for his position: It was from Tampa that the Fernández family controlled the marijuana and cocaine traffic into the United States. At the beginning, when marijuana was transported from South America in fishing boats and transferred to American ships in the Gulf, the operation was relatively simple. Later, with the growing involvement of the Goajiro Indians and organized crime, the business had become much more dangerous.

Santiago found himself entertaining drug pushers, Mafiosi, and American politicians. Lonely and despondent, he found relief in alcohol and barbiturates.

It was eleven-thirty. From the next room came the sounds of the telephone's ring and Nury's whispered reply. Beatrice would be getting up soon. He tried to imagine the face she would make when she heard the news. Would she give him a well-bred look of sympathy? Santiago hoped not.

Outside, in the garden, the breeze had died. In the heat the plants were absolutely still.

Santiago opened the door and took Nury aside. He realized he was imitating his father's tone. "Nury, I'm too upset to handle the arrangements for the funeral. I would appreciate it if you would take care of all the details. You know better than I do what has to be done. I'm sure my father would have wanted a simple burial. See if you can plan it for tomorrow morning." He let go of her arm, smiled sadly, and slipped away before she had a chance to ask any questions.

Beatrice was still asleep, her head under the pillow. Santiago usually avoided waking her, because she tended to start the day in a bad mood; she was, he knew, afraid someone might see her before she'd had a chance to arrange herself in front of the mirror. However, today he was curious to see her response to Villalba's death.

"Beatrice, it's noon," he said. Then, louder: "Beatrice . . ."

She rolled over, hugging the pillow, and opened her eyes. Her brow creased, as if in anger. "What time is it?" she asked, and yawned.

"It's late." He spoke deliberately, calmly. "My father died this morning."

Her eyes opened wide, her face contracted, and she touched his hand. Santiago was pleased; her sympathy seemed unaffected. Despite everything, she was sincere. And she was beautiful.

"Oh, Santiago," she murmured. "That's terrible." Then she looked away. Her tone changed and she whined like a child. "You know I don't like to dress in black."

Santiago laughed and clasped her in his arms. Stroking her back, he felt a tenderness for this self-centered woman that he knew for no one else. "It'll be all right. Don't worry. Nobody is going to make you do anything," he said. "But you have to get up now. We have plans to make."

He heard her sigh deeply. She had fallen back to sleep. He laid her down on the bed; her face was banded by light streaming through the blinds. Santiago peered out and imagined for a moment that he was at the beach with his mother, splashing in the waves, digging for *chipichipis*.

He went into the bathroom and stood in the shower for a long time. The water cleared his mind.

When he came out, Beatrice was awake and eating breakfast in bed from a tray. They chatted while he dressed. She did not mention Villalba's death. She was, in fact, so cheerful that he wondered if sleep had erased the memory.

"Sweetheart," he began, "I'm going to take you to your parents'. I'll drive you myself. I'll be busy most of the day with plans for the funeral, and there's no reason for you to be bothered with any of them. I told Nury to schedule the service for tomorrow morning." He paused to see if she understood. She nodded.

Santiago left her, went downstairs, and took over from Nury, answering the condolence calls himself. Nury had made the arrangements. The body would be on view in the funeral home that night, and early on Ash Wednesday it would be transported to the cathedral. There would be a short, formal religious ceremony. Cardinal Hoyos Calderón himself was traveling from Bogotá to conduct the Mass. Alvaro Villalba, who in his old age had become a devout and generous Catholic, would have been pleased.

He rejoined Beatrice for lunch. They ate in silence. The servants, assuming that grief over Villalba's death had made them too distraught to speak, kept their eyes and voices lowered. Neither Santiago nor Beatrice was dressed in black; as usual, she wore no makeup. Santiago liked her like this—her skin tightened, unblemished, a translucent canvas. Watching her eat chunks of melon, papaya, and pineapple, he marveled at how sad her life had been.

▼ ▼ ▼

When they left for the Fernández's at three, the sky was vibrant, naked, and the sun was blinding. The trees, as if hypnotized by the steaming mist, stood immobile. Santiago turned the car onto the Avenida de la Conquista. A carnival parade was already in progress. As they drove on, both the wild, drunken throng and the traffic grew thicker.

Then a gloved hand reached through the open window on Beatrice's side and let go a handful of white powder. Beatrice screamed. Santiago raised the windows and turned on the air conditioning. He inched the car along. All they could do was hope that the human whirlwind would calm.

The car nosed farther into the crowd, and the powder —lime, he realized, which can burn the eyes—rained hard on the windshield. Santiago turned on the wipers, but the spray mixed with the lime and formed a crusty paste. When Santiago leaned on his horn, the other slow-moving cars joined in. The crowd, irritated, shouted obscenities, and two teenagers jumped on the hood. Santiago got out, but before he could push them off a man wearing a tiger mask flattened him against the door and screamed in his face: "Death to the bourgeoisie!" Santiago threw himself back inside as one of the youths threw lime after him. Beatrice's face was contorted, as if she were trying to shriek, but no sound emerged. A plastic bag hit the windshield, and a yellow liquid ran down the glass. Beatrice's voice burst out: "They're throwing urine. *Dios mio,* Santiago. Help! They're going to kill us."

Rocks hit the car. The glass on Beatrice's side shattered; bits of it fell into her lap. As Santiago reached across her to push away an attacker he saw his wife distractedly pick up the slivers and squeeze them until her fingers and hands became bloody.

The crowd had begun a rhythmic lifting and dropping of the car when a motorcycle cop turned on his siren. The mob suddenly scattered, and the policeman led Santiago and Beatrice a few blocks away and cleaned the windshield. He offered to escort them to the hospital. Santiago, who had seen Beatrice cut herself more dangerously before, assured him that the wounds were not serious. Looking back, the officer shook his head and said, "They're a bunch of savages, sir." Santiago thanked him and drove on.

Beatrice stopped sobbing; her hands were only bleeding lightly now. It was, Santiago thought, as if her body contained only a small quantity of blood. They passed into a part of the city that he didn't know: expansive modernistic houses slumbering behind iron gates— houses that had been built in the last ten years with money from the drug bonanza. Climbing the gentle hills, Santiago drove fast. The ash-gray ocean flashed in the distance. Beatrice sat quietly, absorbed in the sky, staring through the jagged spikes of broken glass at the clouds.

The Fernández home stood at the edge of the city, overlooking the sea highway. The tropical gardens surrounding the two-story house were overgrown with coconut palms. An armed guard was stationed at the gate. Santiago got out of the car. From where he stood one could make out the delta and mouth of the Magdalena River and, farther out, the ocean.

He opened Beatrice's door. With a strange smile on her lips, she extended her hand, dark with blood. Santiago took her in his arms, lifted her out of the car, and carried her to the house. Graciela, her mother, opened the door.

"What happened?" she asked, horrified at the blood. She recovered her composure and added, "Don't let the servants see. Come, we'll go to her room."

Santiago carried his wife up the stairs; she seemed as soft and light as a pillow. The curtains in her bedroom were drawn, and the darkness blinded him for a moment as he laid Beatrice on the bed. Graciela, on her way to telephone the doctor, spun around abruptly, as if remembering something.

"I'm sorry about your father," she said to Santiago. "He's been like a member of our family, too."

Graciela's footsteps faded down the hall, and Santiago turned back to his wife. Her hands had stopped bleeding, but her dress, face, and throat were splotched with blood. He opened the blinds; outside, the day shone brilliant blue. He went out to the small balcony, from which he could see the coconuts, the guava, orange, papaya, tamarind, and almond trees in the garden. Breathing deeply and holding the air in his lungs, he watched a solitary schooner glide by in the distance, its white sail taut against the wind. He went back into the room.

Beatrice was still in a stupor, her face glazed, her eyes puffy from crying. Santiago pulled her to his chest and held her, listening to her heartbeat, so soft at times that it almost seemed to stop. She locked her arms around his neck and promptly dozed off. There were times when the sound of her heart suggested to him the empty hum of a seashell or the pulse of his mother's womb.

The door opened, startling him, and Graciela led the doctor into the room. It was the second time that day Santiago and Dr. Martínez had been together. As Santiago explained what had happened, the physician took a bottle and syringe out of his bag. Taking Beatrice's frail arm, he disinfected the skin, then plunged the needle in. She gasped without waking.

"She'll sleep for a while," he said, withdrawing the needle. "That's good; what she needs most is rest. Now let's take a look at those hands."

After he had gone, Graciela and Santiago undressed Beatrice and tucked her into bed. Graciela bundled up the bloody clothes and left.

Santiago went out to the patio and sat by the pool at an umbrella-shaded table. He called the butler, who, even on carnival Tuesday, was in uniform. Santiago had him bring ice, soda, glasses, and a bottle of scotch. He fixed himself a double on the rocks. He drank it in one gulp, the liquor searing his throat. It was four-thirty. Soon the parade would be over and the last night of carnival could begin. Tomorrow, Ash Wednesday, his father would be buried. He heard steps: His father-in-law, in sunglasses, a white beach towel wrapped around his waist, was walking toward the pool along the winding white stone path.

Santiago stood up.

"Please don't get up," said Antonio, sitting down. "I'm very sorry about your father, sorrier than you . . ." He paused for an interminable few seconds, poured a drink, tasted it, and grimaced; he put in another ice cube. "I knew him before you were born. I was about your age when we met."

Santiago remained silent, idly wondering if Antonio could possibly know the truth about Villalba's death. Santiago usually avoided conversations with Fernández. He suspected that his father-in-law had never liked him, that he had permitted the marriage only because Beatrice had no other suitor.

Antonio leaned back and lit a cigar. He was about fifty, with graying hair, but looked younger. Age had improved his looks, much as age gives gold a richer luster.

Santiago stared at Fernández as if hypnotized and wondered how much longer he could defy the passage of time. Would he put himself in the hands of doctors and clinics as Villalba had done, trying to prolong his life indefinitely? Fernández broke the train of his thoughts, saying, "I've been wanting to talk to you for some time. I have a few things I want to discuss with you." This will end badly, Santiago thought. Still, let's try to keep calm.

"I want to talk to you about your political future," Antonio said. "You are young and inexperienced and there is much that you don't understand. I'm going to give you some advice."

Santiago stared at his father-in-law, showing and saying nothing. Don Antonio Fernández's face was impenetrable and his voice had neither highs nor lows.

"Pardon my frankness, but sometimes it's better just to get to the point," said Antonio, staring back. "You are our creation." He watched for Santiago's reaction. Santiago tried to remain blank. "Yes, you are our creation. Like it or not, we have educated you, married you, and given you your position. We deserve something in return. We want you to have a political career. Stay in Florida at least one more year and I promise that we will either get you into the Senate or find you an ambassadorship. You have lived most of your life outside this country. You don't understand Colombian politics. For better or worse, you're not simply an individual—you represent a whole family. You are about to inherit a considerable fortune, and you are going to have to assume your responsibility to your country and class." Don Antonio paused and took a slow drag on his cigar.

"When we allowed you to marry Beatrice," he went on, peering at Santiago from behind his sunglasses, "when we gave you your first diplomatic post, and later when we had you named consul in Florida, we already knew what we wanted from you."

He was speaking emphatically now. "Listen to me, Santiago. Your father's interests and mine were the same, and still are, now more than ever. You must remember that we have put a lot of money into you. Politics is no game for ungrateful children."

Santiago felt that he couldn't stand any more sermonizing. This conversation could continue some other time. It wasn't right to discuss the future today. He stood up to put an end to the meeting.

"Sit down," Fernández hissed. "I'm not finished yet. Remember that you're in my house. I will tell you when you can go. Show me that with all your education, at least you have some manners!"

Santiago stood there, the glass in his hands, and trembled. He gulped down the contents and took a deep breath. "Is incest good manners?" he asked quietly. "Beatrice has told me all about that."

Antonio was speechless.

Santiago felt suddenly drunk. He turned away and stormed off. He jumped into the car and backed out quickly, nearly slamming into a passing bus. A passenger—probably drunk himself—leaned out of the window and threw a handful of lime; the dust smarted his eyes. Santiago cursed; the car lurched forward and he headed back toward the celebration.

3 ▽

The evening was clear and fresh; the orange full moon already out. When Santiago reached the center of town, he found the city completely alight. The Avenida Olaya Herrera was awash in noisemakers, confetti, broken flowers, and drooling drunks. After four days of festivities, the revelers looked tired but determined to carry on until the last possible moment.

Santiago drove through the packed streets, parked, and got out of the car. At one corner, he let himself be swept into a crowd of people singing, dancing, drinking rum. The merriment was contagious; the Caribbean music and the African drums mesmerized him; the shared bottles of *gordolobo,* plentiful and strong, went to his head. He abandoned himself to the music and joined one of the *comparsas* that danced through the city like Chinese dragons.

▼ ▼ ▼

Hours later, fatigued but exhilarated, Santiago arrived at his father's house. The servants were in the living room watching television, and bottles of *ron caña* were strewn around the room. Embarrassed, Pedro got up to turn off the set, but Santiago stopped him. Since it was carnival, he said grandly, it was all right for them to enjoy themselves. He asked the cook to have dinner sent to his room. In the hall, he picked up the notes and cards that Nury had received that day. One envelope caught his eye—it was an invitation to a party being held that night at the country club to celebrate the end of carnival.

He showered and shaved quickly and returned to his bedroom, where the cook had left a tray of cold cuts. He picked at them absently for a few minutes. Too restless to eat, he suddenly found himself wandering through the hallways of the second floor, opening doors to rooms he barely knew. He walked past the vases full of flowers, the paintings on the walls, and into the bedroom of Lucía, his late half sister.

It was preserved like a room in a museum. The suite, with a private bath and a balcony overlooking the garden, didn't seem as though it belonged to someone who had been dead for fifteen years. There was no dust; everything was spotless and the air was brisk. The room was neat and orderly, as if the servants expected Lucía to arrive any minute.

As a child, Santiago had hated his half sister, thinking of her as the privileged one who had everything he wanted most—especially the love of his father. Many years later he discovered that Lucía, in her own way, had been as unhappy as he.

He looked at the yellowing photographs: Lucía an infant in her mother's arm; Lucía at ten, sitting at the piano; a teenage Lucía playing tennis; Lucía a student at Italian and French conservatories; her debutante ball; her career as a pianist; and finally, two pictures that showed a lovely but prematurely aged woman. It was like this that Santiago remembered her.

One Thursday, while he was at school in Connecticut, Lucía had called him unexpectedly to say that she would be coming to visit him the following Sunday. He was nervous about meeting this sister he had never really known, but when he saw her in the common room in her gray suit, her face sad but wearing a friendly smile, he knew he had nothing to fear. When he took her hand, he noticed it was very white, with long delicate fingers and short fingernails painted rose, the same color as her cheeks. He noticed too her aristocratic air, as if she were a rare orchid who had been kept in a greenhouse all her life. Her soft voice was interrupted occasionally by a rasping cough.

They took a train to New York. It was a cold but clear November afternoon as they strolled through Central Park, crushing dry leaves underfoot, exchanging small talk, still awkward with each other. They had lunch at the Metropolitan Museum. Afterward Lucía took him to visit her favorite room, and they stood for some time caught in a spell in front of the Degas ballerinas. Later, despite the chill, they walked through the park, sat on a bench, and ate ice cream.

They were still sitting there when night fell. Neither wanted to part, but Santiago had to return to school. Lucía took him to Grand Central, and, kissing him on both cheeks, she said goodbye and promised to write. The next day she left for England. The next spring she died in London of cancer.

▼ ▼ ▼

In Lucía's room, Santiago opened the closet and pulled out a dress, gold-flecked and trimmed with feathers. In a drawer he found more feathers, jewelry, sequined shoes, and a blond wig. Still drunk on dancing and *gordolobo,* he tried on the dress, adjusted the wig, and looking in the mirror was astonished by how much he resembled his half-sister. Like her, he was thin, pale-complected, and a bit fragile. He applied makeup, and when he looked in the mirror again he could barely recognize the flapper who stared back.

He crept down the stairs, checking to see if anyone was on the ground floor. There was no one. The servants must have gone to bed, he decided. Wobbly on high heels, he dashed outside to his car.

The city's lights accentuated the desperation of those revelers he passed who wandered the streets looking for something to do. Ash Wednesday would soon surprise the drunks lying in the street. A warm breeze scattered dead leaves and tattered posters. When he arrived at the club, a line of cars was waiting to enter. He was trembling as he handed his invitation to the guard, but the man said, "Good evening," and let him by.

He parked, trying to gather his nerve. Couples were heading for the club and groups of young people were walking toward the golf course. Music blared from the dance hall. He began to perspire. It was one thing for a man to attend a ball on the last day of carnival dressed in black, as a widow of Joselito. Trying to *pass* for a woman was something else. Santiago knew that if he was caught his family would never forgive him. He headed inside.

Once through the terrace entrance, he tottered to the ladies' room, its door pink, covered with streamers. In front of the enormous moon-shaped mirror, he lit a cigarette to steady his trembling hands. He had combed his hair, touched up his makeup, and started out when two girls came through the door. He tried to slip by, but they stopped him. They seemed to be high on something; one of them held a vial in her hands.

"What's your name?" she asked, giggling.

Santiago, afraid that his voice would give him away, stammered.

"I'm Olga," the girl continued, smiling. "Want a line?"

Santiago stared at her. She was beautiful, in a blue gown, with heavy black hair swirling over her bare, tanned shoulders.

"This is Elena," she said, pointing to her friend.

"Hello there." Elena smiled. She looked like Olga, even in the way she was dressed.

Olga took out a silver spoon and opened the glass vial. "Here," she said, moving toward Santiago, giggling. "Ladies first." With a sure hand, Olga put the spoon under Santiago's nose. "Breathe deep," she ordered.

Santiago inhaled. The powder rushed up his nose and penetrated his brain. Olga put the spoon back into the bottle, filled it, and brought it up to his other nostril. He inhaled again and, seconds later, felt the cocaine traveling through his entire body.

"*Es magnífica,*" Olga said.

Santiago nodded his thanks and quickly left, his head buzzing. He could still hear the girls laughing as he breathed the night air. He was nervous, but now, somehow, he felt better.

He minced into the grand ballroom. There seemed to

be hundreds of couples inside, all of them dressed in fabulous costumes, all of them dancing. A waiter offered him a glass of champagne. He sipped it and began to relax when, from the crowd, a man appeared wearing an *antifaz* and asked him to dance. Santiago caught his breath: It was Antonio Fernández, completely drunk. Before he could slip away, his father-in-law put his arms tightly around Santiago's waist and began to sway in rhythm to the samba. He put his lips to Santiago's neck and ground his erection against Santiago's belly. The younger man tried to pull away but was caught in Antonio's grasp; he closed his eyes in resignation and fear. The band took a break and the couples moved toward the free tables. Fernández took Santiago's arm and dragged him to a dark corner.

"Let's go outside," he said, leering.

Santiago pulled away.

"Let's go out and have a good time," Fernández commanded, tightening his grip on Santiago's arm. "I find you totally irresistible."

A group of men in drag appeared from behind the band and began moaning in chorus. "Ay, José, ay José. Don't leave us, José. Don't leave us alone. Don't make us widows," they cried. Some of them wailed and threw themselves on the floor in mock pain. A handful of band members played a funeral dirge.

"Come on," Antonio said. "This is the best time to leave. No one's watching."

Santiago let himself be pulled outside. He could still hear the screaming and the music as Antonio pushed him into a golf cart and steered it up a hill. Through his cocaine haze, Santiago was aware of the couples lying on the grass as he and Antonio whizzed by on the cart.

Fernández stopped. Feeling that this was his last chance to get away before his father-in-law found out who he was, Santiago kicked off his high-heeled shoes and ran. Antonio caught up with him under a tree and grabbed him firmly. They struggled. "You're a strong one, you are," said Fernández. Santiago gave him a yank. The older man pitched forward, his head struck a tree, and he collapsed. Santiago looked at the motionless body in horror and relief.

Gasping, he leaned down and ripped open Antonio's shirt to listen for a heartbeat. When his ear touched Fernández's flesh, he was seized by disgust. He rolled Antonio over and pulled his pants down. Santiago penetrated Fernández quickly and deeply; as his thrusts became faster, he remembered how it had felt to push the pillow into his father's face that morning. He dug his fingernails into Antonio's shoulders, crying out in both rage and pleasure, and came, shuddering. His eyes flew open as he imagined Villalba dying.

At six-thirty in the morning, Santiago, dressed in a gray suit and black tie, parked his car in front of the undertaker's. Until recently, this funeral home, like many others in Barranquilla, had been an imposing private estate. This one featured high white marble columns and wide paths of Arabian tiles. Roses and *lluvias de oro* flourished in manicured beds.

He sat in the car listening to the classical music always played on Ash Wednesday and ran through his mind everything that had happened in the last twenty-four hours. He was exhausted; a long shower and pots of coffee had failed to revive him.

A breeze was coming from the sea, and in the east the sun lingered in the lazy tropical dawn. In a few hours, Santiago thought, after the burial, it will be all over and for the first time I'll be free to live my own life. This line of thought made him feel vaguely inspired. He got out of the car and walked toward the building.

He wasn't looking forward to confronting his father's corpse. It was hard to imagine Alvaro Villalba all made up and ready for the grave. As Santiago walked up the steps, a nearby rooster crowed. The day was beginning.

The main door of the funeral home was ajar. He walked the long, carpeted corridor to the chapel. A large crystal chandelier hung from the ceiling, and the walls were covered with gold-inlaid mirrors. He looked into several rooms, but no one seemed to be in.

Back in the chapel, a cedar casket with heavy brass handles was surrounded by burning candles. Santiago threaded his way through the wreaths that nearly filled the room and approached the coffin. He hoped it would be good to confront his father, that he might thereby rid himself of the haunting memory. He looked inside. There was no corpse. He put his hand out disbelievingly and felt the silk sheets; there was indeed no body. Santiago was certain this was the right funeral home. Maybe he was in the wrong viewing room.

He dashed through the building. All the other rooms were empty. It was a funeral home apparently devoid of corpses. Pacing on the patio, he noticed a small room in the back and walked into it; a chained dog barked furiously. The room was so dark that he had to light a match. Dimly, dimly, he made out a bed and a body curled in a fetal position. He hoped it was Villalba's, then heard a faint snore; it was the undertaker, deep in sleep.

Santiago touched the man's shoulder and pushed him, but he didn't stir. Irritated, Santiago shouted, "Wake up!" and the man's eyes opened. Santiago could see that he was still drunk.

"I am Alvaro Villalba's son," he said sharply. "*¿Dónde está el cadáver de papá?*"

It took the man a few seconds to get his bearings.

"The corpse," repeated Santiago, struggling to suppress his impatience. "Where is my father's corpse?"

"Excuse me, doctor," the undertaker mumbled. "I was—" He began stammering nervously. "The body is over there, in the room," he muttered and stumbled out the door.

Santiago followed his quick lurching steps back into the viewing room from which he had run moments before. The man walked to the casket, looked inside, jumped back, and whispered, "*¡Dios mio!* They've stolen Señor Villalba's body."

Santiago's first impulse was to slap him. He lit a cigarette instead. "Who the hell would do that?"

"Today is Ash Wednesday," came the response.

Santiago remembered: It was an Ash Wednesday custom for children to place rag dolls in small coffins and carry them from door to door, crying over the death of Joselito Carnaval and begging for coins with which to bury the dead. Someone with a perverse sense of humor might have stolen the body to carry it through the city. The thought outraged him. "I'll have you arrested," he barked at the man.

The undertaker hurried to Santiago and knelt before him. "Please forgive me, doctor. *Por favor, doctorcito.*"

"Forgive you! Where is the phone? I'm calling the police."

The man grabbed his hand. "No, please, doctor," he begged. "We will find Don Alvaro. I'm sure they'll return the body. I beg you, don't call the police."

Santiago's thoughts were racing. "In a few minutes, they'll come to take the body to church." He paused. "If anyone ever finds out about this, I'll see to it that you and your family are ruined."

The man remained on his knees. He was trembling.

"Get up," said Santiago. "Come with me."

He walked into the hall, through the house, and onto the patio. "What's in those bags?" he asked, pointing to a pile on the ground underneath a cashew tree.

"Cement, doctor. For construction that—"

Santiago cut him off. "Help me," he said and bent to lift a heavy bag. Five minutes later they had dragged four bags into the viewing room, put them into the coffin, and locked it shut. Santiago went into the bathroom to wash his hands. The man, still terrified, stood with his head hanging.

"What's your name?" he called from the sink.

"Rodríguez. Jorge Rodríguez, at your service, doctor."

"Listen, Rodríguez," Santiago said, drying his hands and taking some bills from his wallet. "Take this. Keep quiet and nothing will happen."

The man's eyes lit up when he saw the money. Santiago heard a car pull up. Peering through the blinds, he watched four men get out and climb the stairs. A few minutes later they were carrying the coffin to the car. The hearse pulled away; Santiago waved to Rodríguez and got into his own car. The day had begun; the sun was burning though the tropical mist.

Waiting for a traffic light to change, he saw a group of children with ash crosses on their foreheads carrying a mock coffin. Santiago toyed with the idea that in it lay Villalba's body. He watched the children until the driver behind him honked.

Minutes later, Santiago reached the church. The street was full of cars, and passersby were lined up on the sidewalks, ogling the mourners. He searched the crowd for Beatrice and her family, spotting her father first. Antonio Fernández, dressed in black, seemed perfectly at ease, as if nothing unusual had happened the night before. Santiago joined the group, and Beatrice took his arm. They entered the church to the clicking of photographers' cameras.

The modern but opulent cathedral was choked with irises and yellow roses. The coffin had been placed in front of a huge crucifix. Santiago and the Fernández family took their places in the first pew. The church was full; Santiago felt hundreds of eyes staring at him.

Cardinal Hoyos Calderón conducted a brief Mass; his voice was charged with emotion as he recalled the deceased's charity. Alvaro Villalba was "a pillar of strength and integrity, a fountain of generosity, a man of God," according to the cardinal.

When he offered communion, Santiago got up—much to Beatrice's surprise—and led the other mourners to the altar.

The cardinal gave him a wafer and traced the sign of the cross on his forehead. Santiago closed his eyes and silently, for the first time in years, prayed—he wasn't sure for what. When he returned to his seat, Beatrice was looking at him with amazement in her eyes.

Organ music thundered, and the mourners dispersed.

Behind the hearse, his father's black Mercedes was waiting. Pedro opened the door. Beatrice lay back and rested her head on her husband's shoulder.

Santiago wanted to be alone with his thoughts. As the procession began to move, led by police cars with sirens blaring, he smiled to himself, thinking how different his life would be from now on. He was finally free of his father—completely, irrevocably free.

They entered the cemetery, its cultivated tombless gardens watched over by a marble Christ. The hearse stopped at a newly dug grave and the casket was removed. Before he opened the door, Beatrice looked into Santiago's eyes and said softly, "I don't understand how the body—"

Santiago was barely aware she was speaking. He stroked her hair. "Don't worry about anything, darling."

In the moist, black soil, worms were still trying to make their way into the coolness below. He took his wife's hand and gazed out at the horizon. The blue of the sky was punctuated by the white of a yacht's sails and the gray of a tugboat. To Santiago, the forms seemed to be emerging as if from a dream.

"But what I want to know is how the coffin—"

He wouldn't let her finish. "Not now," he said, squeezing her hand. "We can talk later. We have our whole lives ahead of us."

II
BOGOTÁ

Bogotá is high and cold and wet, a damp chill that gets inside you like the inner cold of junk sickness.

WILLIAM BURROUGHS,
The Yage Letters, 1963

4 ▽

Antonio Fernández had been Alvaro Villalba's partner and lawyer, and in recent years had taken over the administration of Villalba's interests. Now, Fernández informed Santiago that the inheritance papers were being filed, that he would be receiving a letter outlining his holdings, and that a bank account in Bogotá was available to him in the interim. Although aware that his decision would upset his father-in-law, Santiago quit his post in Tampa and moved with his wife into the duplex penthouse in Bogotá that had belonged to his father.

Surrounded by hanging gardens, this building bordered the Plaza de Toros and offered astonishing views of the savannah and mountains. Beatrice fell in love with the apartment; in an effort to exorcise his father's presence, Santiago encouraged her to redecorate it.

The Bogotá of his childhood had changed. The old city had been colonial, cold and gray, rooted in the European cultures that had founded it. The old ways still remained, but they now existed alongside the symbols of American modernization. Burros, cows, and horses roamed freely over manicured avenues; cardboard hovels clustered by skyscrapers.

Though he did not yet know the terms of his inheritance, Santiago suspected it would be so large he would never again have to worry about money. After a few months of loafing, he was thoroughly bored. Santiago, who had spent so much time abroad, felt like an exile in his native land.

Beatrice, on the other hand, improved remarkably, and made no more suicide attempts. When she began to talk about having a child, the couple decided to return to New York, where medical care was better. Santiago remembered a spacious apartment in the Olympic Towers that his father had bought as an investment a few years before and arranged for them to stay there.

For months they lived in idle luxury. Beatrice went to consult the best specialists; the doctors suggested that since she and Santiago had not had sex for some time, Beatrice be artificially inseminated. Santiago was relieved and happy to leave his sperm in a glass vial. As Beatrice had become more and more like an adored child to him his desire for her had waned.

At a Christmas party given by Venezuelan friends, Santiago noticed a man eyeing him intently. He would stare and then blink half a dozen times or so. Observing him for a few minutes it became apparent that this was a nervous tic. His hands were in constant motion as he spoke. When the man moved among the guests, Santiago noticed he dragged his left leg stiffly behind him. Late in the evening, when the crowd began to thin out, the stranger approached him.

"Santiago, don't you know who I am? You're as out of it as ever! Mario Simán."

Almost twenty years had gone by since Santiago had seen his childhood friend. He smiled and hugged him warmly.

Mario's father had become the president of Colombia and Mario was now an international pre-Columbian art collector. He took Santiago to the galleries and auctions. Several weeks later when Mario announced his imminent return to Colombia, he presented Santiago with two magnificent pre-Columbian gold *tunjos* as a token of their rekindled friendship.

Santiago promised Mario a visit, but it wasn't until he received several urgent calls from Antonio Fernández that he made plans to go. He was extremely apprehensive about this trip; he knew his father's corpse waited there for him somewhere. Fernández had indicated that business problems were pressing. Resolving once and for all to end his financial ties to Fernández, Santiago agreed to a meeting in Bogotá. He left Beatrice in New York under her doctor's care and booked a flight for the first Sunday in February.

As the plane began its descent into the El Dorado Airport, Santiago wondered how the Spanish conquistadores could have negotiated the steep, narrow Andes path. From above, the mountains looked impossibly treacherous.

He got through customs quickly and found the driver waiting for him. They drove off in the black Mercedes, past fields overflowing with summer wildflowers, and with tall, forever-green *urapanes*.

When they reached the penthouse at about six that evening, the housekeeper greeted him politely, but with reserve. Santiago knew that this woman, who together with her husband, the driver, had been absolute master of the apartment during his absence, felt his arrival to be an intrusion. He made a mental note to get rid of both of them as soon as possible. They had worked for his father for more than thirty years, and Santiago was certain they considered him a usurper. Besides, they were another link to a past he wanted to bury.

Standing in the living room, he took in the warmth of the sunlight as it baked the apartment and the exuberance of the potted fuchsias. Santiago seemed to remember the place only vaguely; even when he and Beatrice had lived there it had never really felt like home.

Santiago poured himself a cognac and went out to the terrace. A fresh breeze blew in the dying afternoon. The sky seemed a huge Technicolor screen with different layers of clouds playing out a drama of light: the first layer lead gray; the second, a few hundred feet above the savannah, like a belly painted pink; the sky itself ultramarine; and the darkness overhead like octopus ink, seeping through. Turning around, he looked at the mountains: They seemed to have been placed there in deliberate counterpoint to the architectural landscape. Above, Venus shone like a diamond, and the moon—a turtle egg about to hatch—stood poised over the chapel of Monserrate, its lighted tower floating in the dusk like a spaceship about to descend.

When the wind turned chilly, he went inside, dialed the operator, and asked her to place a call to Fernández in Barranquilla. He was not altogether surprised when, four hours later, the call had not gone through. He gave up and went to bed.

▼ ▼ ▼

He awoke at dawn to cries that seemed to come from the living room. At first he was alarmed; then he remembered that sometimes during the bullfights, nearby buildings absorbed the cheers and groans of the spectators, and released them much later. He stayed in bed in the dark for a while and listened to the *bravos* and *olé toreros* rise and ebb like rhythmic waves.

He got up, put on his robe, and stood at the bedroom window. The powerful spotlights of the Plaza de Toros cast an orange light through the heavy mist; Santiago could see the sandy arena, speckled with blood from bulls killed the previous afternoon.

He shuddered as he remembered the last time he had seen a bullfight. He was seven years old and with his mother. The crowd had booed and hissed the dictator's daughter, an overripe thirty-eight-year-old whose father had had her crowned Miss Colombia. To punish the hissers, the dictator ordered the army to lock all of the arena's exit doors. For five days the crowd remained trapped, while soldiers singled out young people they believed to be intellectuals and shot them. Hearing the crowd's familiar cries now, Santiago felt that he was still in that bullring, hugging his mother and witnessing the massacre, smelling the stench of shit, piss, and rotting bodies.

The rain fell harder, and as the water diluted the blood, crimson puddles spread over the ring; under the spotlights, they became red mirrors. The *olés* continued. He went into the bathroom, where he discovered that he had an erection. Santiago stood in the middle of the room and masturbated, his mind a blank. He swallowed two barbiturates and washed them down with a shot of cognac. The next thing he knew it was noon and the telephone was ringing. His father-in-law had arrived in Bogotá; he told Santiago to meet him that night in the Chibcha Room of the Guatavita Hotel. The tone of Fernández's voice suggested that the evening would be an unpleasant one.

At eight, Santiago walked to downtown Bogotá. He was nervous. Fernández had never mentioned the night at the country club, but Santiago couldn't be sure he did not know what had happened, or with whom. He also knew Fernández would try to pressure him. He crossed the Carrera Séptima and went through the main lobby of the hotel to the elevator, which took him to the top floor. The Chibcha Room was empty, and Don Antonio was nowhere in sight.

Santiago sat down at a table beside a glass wall, lit his cigarette in the candle flame, and ordered a straight vodka. He didn't want to drink the water in Bogotá until his stomach was accustomed to the food again; during his last visit, he had come down with a case of amoebic dysentery that had taken him months to shake off.

Antonio Fernández arrived several minutes later. He looked younger than ever; his weight was down, and he had the lithe step of an adolescent. He wore a deep-blue three-piece suit, alligator shoes, and a white silk shirt; his pearl-gray tie was pinned with a ruby. They shook hands warily. Antonio sat down and ordered a mineral water. "I'm not drinking anymore. It ages you," he said, scrutinizing Santiago. "How's Beatrice?"

Santiago suddenly realized that Antonio never called Beatrice "my daughter"; it was always "Beatrice," as if this formality distanced him from her problems.

"She's fine. Great. She loves New York."

"When I was young, I traveled a lot, too," Antonio said. "Of course, in those days, it wasn't as easy as it is now. But I don't really approve of living abroad permanently."

"Beatrice is used to living abroad because you sent her away when she was a child."

Antonio ignored the accusation and sipped his mineral water. "We have a lot to talk about."

Santiago turned away and looked through the window at the traffic below. When he turned back, Antonio's face was determined. "Your father and I spent our whole lives working for the future of our children. I'm disappointed that you left your consular post. It's shameful."

"I'm not interested in diplomacy," Santiago shot back.

There was a ferocious glint in Antonio's black eyes. "I'd like to know what *does* interest you."

Santiago would have liked to tell him the truth: His life's ambition had been to get revenge on his father. After smothering him and getting away with it, he had experienced only a profound emptiness. Although Santiago was perfectly aware that Antonio was trying to rattle him, he could feel his resolution to stay in control falter. He sipped his vodka. "Maybe in the future I'd like to—"

"The future! What the hell does that mean? The future, indeed. You must take an interest in your holdings." He sighed and began again. "I want you to open an export office in Bogotá, Santiago. I've already asked Mario Simán to show you around. Your father and I were co-owners of two *fincas*—rather large ones. Very fertile.

I called you down because we need to discuss their administration."

"What kind of *fincas*?" asked Santiago. He would try to be civil for the rest of the meeting.

"Years ago they were banana plantations."

"But the banana business is—"

Antonio interrupted impatiently. "I said years ago." He paused.

"Your father made his fortune farming bananas. The two great passions of his life were banana farming and cockfighting. But since the business collapsed those farms have produced nothing but debts. Alvaro wouldn't let them go."

"Why don't we sell them?" Santiago suggested. "Why keep land that has no value?"

"Let me spell it out for you. Fifteen years ago, Alvaro was in bad financial trouble; he had been losing great sums on banana harvests. But he was stubborn. He took bank loans, sold cattle, property, stocks, anything—except his fighting cocks, of course. Those farms had irreplaceable sentimental value to him; you wouldn't remember but you lived on one with Isadora as a child. Finally, they had to be mortgaged, and if I hadn't helped out, they would have been lost. That's why I'm now a co-owner."

"And the farms are still losing money?" asked Santiago, who was getting interested in the conversation.

"No, not anymore. Now they're making a very nice profit."

Santiago was confused. He knew that his inheritance was not the legacy of a man close to bankruptcy.

Antonio paused and sipped his mineral water. Now that he had Santiago's attention, he would tease him.

"We had to change crops. Oh, we continued to grow bananas so your father wouldn't die of grief. But we . . . diversified." He smiled to himself.

"What do you mean, 'diversified'?"

"Rice, cotton, marijuana," Antonio said lazily. The last word came out just a little more smoothly and slowly than the others.

Santiago had seen it coming. It was common knowledge that the Fernández family was in the marijuana business, but he hadn't known it was grown on his father's land. "In other words," he asked, "they are marijuana plantations now?"

"Not so loud. No need to announce it to the help," Antonio said, finishing his mineral water in one gulp. His delicate fingers—the pinky adorned with an oversized Muzo emerald ring—drummed on the tablecloth. "Let's say it's the main crop, the main source of income. Why, since 1974, the entire country has cultivated more marijuana than coffee. We cannot sell those farms."

Santiago had finished his drink. He signaled to the waiter and ordered another vodka.

"Let me give you some advice," Antonio said. "If you are going to drink vodka, drink Wyborowa—that's what civilized people drink."

Santiago nodded to the waiter. After he had gone, Santiago said, "I'd rather sell my share. I'm not interested in the drug business."

Antonio leaned threateningly across the table. "You're not selling anything, understand?"

The waiter returned with the drink, and Santiago whispered, "You don't need that money. You already have more than enough."

"When you grow up," Antonio said, "you'll understand that there's no such thing as too much money."

"Why don't you buy me out of the farms? I'll sell at a good price. I just don't want to get involved in drug dealing."

Antonio frowned. "I could buy them if I wanted to. But there's such a thing as family tradition. What's wrong with you? A family can't fall apart because one member won't play ball. You cannot betray the Villalbas and refuse your responsibilities." He looked away, his eyes drinking in the darkness of the night, then looked back.

Santiago tasted the vodka; Antonio was right, it was better. "I don't like illegal businesses," Santiago said.

Fernández looked as though he would burst. "It's a perfectly respectable business. The best families in the country are involved. The government is on our side! This is not something you can just ignore. You know, this prosperity won't last forever. Bananas were our main crop for decades—now look at them. The marijuana business will dry up sooner or later, I'm afraid, but right now it's a gold mine. You never know what can happen in a country like this. There could be a coup next month. You've learned to live well, Santiago. It's not so easy to get used to less." His index finger tapped on the table in rhythm to his words. "How do you suppose the generals keep up their life-style? We're the ones who support them. Even Washington is involved."

"Did my father know about this?"

"Your father was senile, and he left that part of the business up to me. Alvaro was my father's best friend, and after my father's death we became partners. Alvaro was so pious and gave so much money to the church that people thought he was a saint. But those who knew him . . . He wasn't so nice to your mother or to you, was he?"

Santiago shivered. "I just don't want to make things more complicated for myself, you know."

Antonio patted Santiago's hand. "There is nothing complicated about it. Marijuana is a clean, decent business, not like cocaine and the rest; they attract bad people. Marijuana belongs in the hands of the old landowning class. Once you've been in the business, you can't just get out."

"But I've never been involved in the business," protested Santiago.

"Don't talk nonsense, Santiago. Of course you have. You were consul in Florida when we were starting to traffic in large quantities. You helped open the market. These plantations belong to you—at least, half of them do—and they have been producing the best marijuana in the world for the last fifteen years. But unless we're careful, we may lose out to Mexico, Thailand, even the States; right now they're producing excellent grass in California, Florida, and Pennsylvania, and it looks as if they might legalize it. If they do that, it's all over. You want to see a dirty business? Look at the Americans and their heroin! Santiago, I need someone—someone in the family—to operate the Bogotá office."

The subject of drugs had brought Antonio to life; his eyes were shining and he was trembling. Santiago found his father-in-law's plea almost touching. "I need to think about this," Santiago said. He stood up.

"I hope you understand what I'm saying. Ignorance and innocence are not the same thing. You're in this, whether you like it or not. You had better take the responsibility. Despite what you may think, it's a privilege to be a member of our class. Perhaps you have lived abroad too long to know about the responsibilities that accompany the privileges, but you will learn. *Noblesse oblige,* my boy, *noblesse oblige.*"

Santiago reached for the check.

"It's on me," his father-in-law said. "After all, you're like my own son."

As Antonio paid, Santiago wondered how much this man knew about his father's death, about the corpse. He thought about the incestuous relationship that had deranged Beatrice. He wished now that he had murdered Fernández that night on the golf course.

5 ▽

When the doorman offered to flag a taxi, Santiago didn't
bother to answer; one thing he had learned from his
father was that in Colombia there is no need to be polite
to one's inferiors. He crossed the street and headed
south toward the center of town. Noisy old buses clat-
tered by, filled with passengers who hung from the doors
and windows. It was a clear February night; the nearby
mountains loomed in dark profile. In the park, stumpy
Andean palms grew among ferns like prehistoric trees,
and the lustrous shivering eucalyptus leaves gleamed
silver.

Santiago felt nauseated—it always took him a few
weeks to get used to the change in altitude. As he
walked, he pondered his legacy—a barren, demented
wife, the drug empire he shared with a father-in-law he
despised, and the torturous image of the father he had
killed. He felt disoriented. His head was spinning. He

straightened up. He didn't want people to think he was another drunk staggering through the streets.

Santiago was more familiar with Paris and New York than Bogotá. He turned onto the Carrera Séptima, the spine of downtown. For someone who had lived abroad, entering Bogotá was like stepping into a time machine. Tall, narrow buildings stood at attention like soldiers in the half-empty streets. Indian women, wrapped in heavy dark *ruanas,* lingered on corners, shielding scuzzy disheveled children from the cold. "Mal . . . boro, Mal . . . boro," they chanted.

Undernourished teenagers in rags hunched on the sidewalks like relics of the past, their eyes bloodshot from drugs and malnutrition. Dirty blankets were spread with trinkets for sale—leather goods, small color prints of the saints, posters of politicians and movie stars. Only a handful of passersby emerging from their office buildings and restaurants were well dressed; and they hailed cabs or quickly walked through the poorly lit streets to the avenue.

The more he walked the dizzier he became. The fog billowed like smoke, burying his feet as he passed record shops blaring salsa and rock. Cripples leaned against cement-block walls, their hands and faces eaten away by leprous sores. Smudge-faced barefoot children approached him for money. Although their clothes were tattered, they all wore ties. Older children, small as pygmies, carried infants and toddlers on their backs; their heads seemed to float above the fog. Santiago observed them with curiosity, offering them nothing.

Turning a corner, he saw the transvestites. Flamboyant in dress and manner, many of them more beautiful than the most beautiful women, they ambled along, throwing come-hither looks at older men in business suits.

The fog rolled down from the mountains, creeping forward like a regiment of silent spirits. A legless beggar, balanced on a sweeper's cart, wheeled to stop in front of Santiago. He offered the man a twenty peso coin. The beggar refused it, spat on his leg, and pursued him through the mist. Santiago could barely see, but he could hear the screeching the cart made on the pitted, shit-spattered sidewalk. Santiago broke into a run and quickly outdistanced the awful noise. He felt he had stumbled into a medieval culture. Gasping for breath, he slowed to a walk. *Locos,* despite the cold, splashed naked in the fountain of a plaza. Haggard-faced policemen walked in pairs, stopping pedestrians to check their papers.

Farther on, Santiago passed a group of soldiers, as still as statues, clutching bayonetted rifles. He walked past dozens of policemen and soldiers without being stopped, his expensive clothes the key to their trust. A heavy war tank heading north on the Carrera Séptima broke through a charcoal cloud. On top of the tank a stone-faced soldier flashed a Thompson machine gun.

The cold grew bitter and the rumble of tanks grew louder. Small boys crouched in doorways and lay on the sidewalks, covered with newspapers and cardboard, piled one on top of another to keep warm. Beggars rifled garbage pails for food, and planted themselves in the paths of passersby, blocking their way and begging for *pan* and money.

In the few restaurants still open, men huddled over steaming cups of coffee as the fog took possession of the street. Santiago was tired and began looking for a cab but realized he was in a part of town where taxis didn't come at that hour. He stood in the drizzle for twenty minutes. When a car finally pulled up, he got in, but the driver, on hearing the address, said he wouldn't be able to make it up the hill. Santiago got out; the taxi lurched away.

The rain fell frigid and biting.

Santiago was still waiting on the deserted street corner, feeling like a fool, when a pair of headlights emerged from the fog. A shiny black Mercedes braked to a stop a few yards from him. A familiar voice came from inside. "Santiago, what the fuck are you doing here?"

It was Mario Simán, whom he hadn't seen since New York. As Santiago pulled open a rear door, he felt something tug at his left arm; two small boys had snatched his watch, then leaped like deer into the night. A huge man jumped out of Mario's car and fired a revolver in the boys' direction.

"Skip it," Mario ordered. "Let's go."

The chauffeur put the car in gear, ignoring the red light at the intersection. In the backseat, next to Mario, sat a young woman.

"Caridad," Mario said, "I'd like you to meet Santiago Villalba. I've been hoping to get you two together for a while now, but I never expected it to be here."

Caridad smiled; her teeth were a necklace of small pearls. "Pleased to meet you," she said. "Mario has told me a lot about you." Auburn curls fell to her shoulders. Her skin was glossy and flushed, her jade eyes were ringed by long, abundant lashes, and her features were delicate.

The car raced through the mist twisting up the mountain. The driver parked in front of a metal sentry box that housed an armed guard. Caridad and Mario led Santiago to a high red-brick wall. Immense ferns hid a wooden door. Mario pressed a button, a sharp buzz rang out, and he pushed the door open. Bending down to avoid the low branches, they climbed a stone path. On the left, pre-Columbian statues stood in terraced gardens; on the right, half a dozen brightly colored pheasants and a bird of paradise slept in a bronze cage.

The rain had stopped, and the mountain slopes were free of the fog that enveloped the city below. Santiago was completely sober but still shaken. The moon shone silver over the mountains. It looked like a Ping-Pong ball. They climbed steps flanked by white and pink orchids and arrived at the front door. A sleepy young maid opened it and took their coats. She led them through hallways decorated with luminous paintings of the savannah to a small room. Inside, on a black Formica table, stood small pre-Columbian sculptures. Four enormous Chibchan urns, silent guards, flanked a glassed-in garden. The walls of the living room were covered with black wool. Hanging on them was Mario's collection of pre-Columbian gold.

Santiago and Caridad sat down, and Mario knelt at the fireplace. The maid returned with a liquor caddy, then left, dragging her feet with fatigue.

As Mario lit a fire, Santiago studied Caridad. She couldn't have been more than twenty-five, yet there was something older about her. She was slender, with a small waist and long legs, and wore black leather pants, spike heels, and a lavender silk blouse open at the neck, revealing ivory breasts. She was covered in gold. At her neck hung a layered collar of polished reddish *tuma* stones with miniature gold turtles, frogs, a Tairona nose pendant, and a coral clasp. Around her right arm, half-way between wrist and elbow, curled a gold bracelet in the shape of a snake, with emeralds for eyes. Her sharp black-painted fingernails were set off by Calima rings. Santiago thought he detected something cruel and harsh in her demeanor.

Santiago lay back on the sofa and stroked its fur cushions. He felt oddly excited by what the evening might bring.

The logs caught fire, flames leaped up, and Mario turned to Santiago. "What the hell were you doing in the streets? Didn't you see the cops crawling all over the place? You know there's a curfew."

"It was still early when I left the hotel," he answered, a little embarrassed. "The weather was nice, and I wanted to take a walk and look around. The truth is that I don't know Bogotá very well."

"We could see that," Caridad said sarcastically, taking off her shoes and curling up like a cat in the armchair. Her feet were small, white, and perfect.

"Wise up. Bogotá ain't New York. You're in Colombia." Mario began mixing drinks.

"*Caca*-lombia," corrected Caridad with a teasing smile.

"And she should know," Mario said. "She's chief of PAX, the Colombian secret police."

"Really?" asked Santiago.

Caridad smiled.

Mario set vodka martinis in front of his friends.

Caridad sipped her drink. "I'm not a bit hungry. Let's have some fun. Santiago must be used to a more interesting kind of nightlife. This place is the pits—if it weren't for the opera and the embassy parties, I'd die of boredom." She stood up and walked toward the record player. "Can I play Tito Puente?" she asked Mario.

"Why not?" Mario walked to a room at the end of the hall and returned a minute later holding a small gold box.

Caridad gave a sigh of relief.

Mario glanced at Santiago. "Want to powder your nose?"

He nodded, although it had been a long time since he had used cocaine. Using a delicate gold spoon, Mario poured the white powder from the box onto a large disc of Quimbaya gold. Caridad and Santiago watched him separate the cocaine into portions with a knife. When Mario had made a dozen long thin rows, he took a new bill, rolled it into a straw, and put one end to the gold disc and the other to his right nostril. He inhaled deeply. "Umm . . . fabulous," he hummed.

Santiago took his turn last. He felt nothing at first, but the third line gave his head a cool, electric rush. He snorted one more line, closed his eyes, and for an instant thought he could see his own brain floating in space, the blood vessels filled with liquid, platinum cocaine.

When he opened his eyes, he saw Caridad and Mario sprinkling cocaine on the tips of their tongues. He did the same, and as his tongue, his lips, and the roof of his mouth went numb he suddenly felt better than he had for months. The flames in the fireplace, the shimmering gold, the rain outside, and the tropical music all seemed to whirl inside his head.

Caridad stood up to dance, oblivious of the two men. Hips swaying, she lost herself in the rhythm of the song.

Mario stood up and took her in his arms. Santiago felt his own erection as he watched the couple kiss passionately. Soon they stopped dancing and, with arms around each other's waists, left the room.

A dizzying chill shook Santiago's body. He turned the record over and poured himself a straight vodka. As he sipped it, tears came to his eyes; another drink and two more lines of cocaine soothed him. He walked around the room, caressed the ancient objects with the tips of his fingers, picked up a grotesque gold mask and placed it on his face. Transported, he took off his clothes and put on breast and shoulder ornaments, arm bands, golden anklets, leg pieces, a nose plug, and a feather crown and cape. Raising a golden rattle and scepter over his head, he looked at his reflection in the window and said aloud, "I *am* El Dorado."

Laughing insanely to himself, he set off in search of his friends and found himself in the kitchen. A guard listening to the radio and drinking *aguardiente* gave Santiago a bewildered look, exclaimed, "*¡Ave María!*" and crossed himself. A Doberman threw itself against the iron gate on the patio, barking hoarsely and baring its sharp fangs.

Santiago hurried back to the living room, then went up the stairs, opening door after door until he found a bedroom where candlelight and rock music ricocheted off the walls. Mario and Caridad were naked on a round bed.

In the dark, he stepped on an object and stumbled.

"Watch out for my leg!" Mario shouted.

Santiago stood next to the bed and stared down at them.

Caridad laughed and held out her arms. "Come to me, my golden man."

She removed the gold piece by piece. Santiago dropped the feather cape on the floor, took off his mask, and smiled as he got into bed. Watching the reflection of their bodies in the smoky glass ceiling, Santiago felt a warm moist tongue draw back his foreskin.

The next afternoon, Mario and Santiago and two body-guards left for Santa Marta in Mario's private plane. It was a short trip—barely forty minutes before the plane touched down at a small airport near the ocean. A wait-ing car drove them to El Rodadero. The immense burn-ing sun was hanging low in the horizon when the car dropped them near the narrow wooden pier where Ma-rio's boat, a pure-white yacht, was anchored. Its flag displayed a Chibcha mask.

The two friends sat down on deck chairs to drink mar-tinis. The tide was coming in and dark waves lapped the shore. Flocks of pelicans and sea ravens were flying to-ward their nesting islands. The ship began to move; the wind was bittersweet.

The yacht moored at a wharf of barnacle-covered tim-bers. The island was a gigantic ocher-colored rock whose only vegetation was cacti. On top of it stood an enormous glass building. Thousands of iridescent min-nows darted here and there as Mario and Santiago clam-bered onto a stone terrace and climbed half a dozen narrow steps to a glass elevator; it rose slowly.

They stepped off. The atrium was vast, with bridges crossing brooks full of algae, fish, crabs, and snails.

Mario was obviously pleased to be able to show his house off and gave Santiago the tour. Black marble staircases led from one level to another. Ferns hung from the ceilings and grew voluptuously throughout. On the second floor, in the center of an empty room, was a gold cage big enough to hold condors. Inside it were rocks, trees, fountains, and birds of rainbow plumage. To Santiago, the house suggested a primitive shrine.

Mario led Santiago out onto the terrace for more cocktails. The horizon was a long, thin, fiery coil. Salmon rivulets rippled on the serene Caribbean surface.

Around nine, a helicopter emerged from the darkness and landed on one of the lower terraces; Mario had ordered dinner to be brought in from Martinique. Two lean young waiters dressed in red *guayaberas* served them langouste and Dom Perignon and Santiago half listened as Mario talked about his latest pre-Columbian finds. Then Mario took Santiago to the observatory.

A gold tray heaped with cocaine was waiting for them. Santiago couldn't hide his surprise—he had never imagined using the drug in such large quantities. "Couldn't we smoke pot instead?" he asked.

Mario frowned. "Smoke is for peasants, man. Chill out. This is what they have for breakfast in Hollywood—champagne and cocaine. How do you think the Incas built Machu Picchu? They weren't eating potatoes." He laughed and began to cut the cocaine into lines. "Colombia's not so bad . . . if daddy's President."

"This kind of wealth . . ." Santiago began.

"Being President here is no big deal," Mario interrupted. "This isn't a country—it's a big farm with a few conveniences. In a real country if you get bored in the afternoon, you can go to a museum that has Picasso at least."

Santiago sipped his vodka, dragged on his cigarette, and said nothing. Mario inhaled more cocaine, then stared into his friend's eyes. "Santiago, don't be such a gringo bore. This place is like ancient Egypt; we're the pharaohs and those dumbfuck peasants do the building for us. Don't forget, you're a bastard, you know. It wasn't that long ago that bastards were untouchables." His mood suddenly changed. "Do you know how I lost my leg?" he asked.

Santiago knew the story but didn't interrupt.

"My father was Minister of Foreign Affairs, right? But he made me take the bus to school. Some democratic idea of his. Well, one day I missed the bus and papa had the chauffeur take me in the limo. As soon as he turned on the ignition, the car blew up. The driver went through the windshield and flew fifty feet before he died. I was lucky. I only lost my leg." Mario sipped his vodka.

Santiago murmured, "I'm sorry."

"Do you know the stories they tell about me?" Mario asked, as if he hadn't heard. "They say I killed hundreds of people until I found the perfect leg to graft. You know, they even say I have crematoriums in this place." He smiled painfully and ran his hand over his face and through the curls of his hair. "That's why, when I deal with people, I remember what they know—or think they know—about me. I'm lucky to be the President's son. You're lucky to be so rich."

Santiago started. "I'm not that rich."

Mario blinked his eyes in disbelief. "Santiago, do you

see these islands?" he asked, drawing a semicircle to indicate the expanse of the bay. "Half of them belonged to your old man. Now they belong to you. Haven't you ever looked at your inheritance papers?"

Santiago stared into the open darkness. The cocaine seemed to have emptied his head. "I guess there is a lot Antonio hasn't told me." The sound of his own voice surprised him more than Mario's news.

"Antonio is a puritan with a cross up his ass. He belongs to that same old Spanish aristocracy that your father did. Once in a while they may be extravagant, buy a Zurbarán, a house in Mayfair, or even a Gothic cathedral; but deep down they're really cheapskates. Antonio comes from money and likes to live the good life, but he doesn't blow his cash unless he gets something back. You know what they say about an idle mind being the devil's playground." Mario paused.

Santiago pretended not to understand. "You mean the drug business?"

"You got the picture," Mario said ironically. "Hang around Santa Marta for a few days, I'll really open your eyes."

They had consumed most of the cocaine when the clock on the wall struck three. A circular, grotesquely enlarged moon lit the landscape with its milky light. From the terrace, they saw schools of dolphins breaking the mirror of the sea.

Mario's voice caught Santiago's attention. "We're much too coked up to sleep. How about going fishing?" he asked, standing up. Strangely, fishing seemed at that moment the most interesting idea in the world.

They fished until dawn, when the stars dropped out of the sky and sank in the horizon. The sun rose. Lifting anchor, they turned back, followed by a school of sharks. Mario took out an automatic rifle and began shooting until several sharks bled; the others, crazed by the scent, began to devour them, turning the water bloody with intestines, fins, and jawbones.

Santiago woke up hours later in the glass house with clotted blood blocking his nostrils and drenching his pillow. As he staggered to the bathroom, the sun was setting behind Mario Simán's island.

It was in the coastal town of Santa Marta that Simón Bolívar died cursing Colombia; he had liberated the country from the Spanish, and it had repaid him by throwing him in prison. And, over a century later, it was in Alvaro Villalba's Santa Marta office that Santiago had been received on his yearly visits. The town hadn't been much more than a hamlet then, with one main street running the length of the bay and only a few motels, all of them built at the beginning of the century, facing the water. But by the early 1960s, sewage and seafaring traffic had left Santa Marta's bay a pool of thick oil and entrepreneurs had moved north to the town of El Rodadero, which quickly became a high-rise-cluttered vacation resort.

The major drug traffickers of the area had begun operating out of El Rodadero. At midnight, every night, the waters of the bay would light up with the beacons of arriving boats. Caravans of trucks would meet them, and strong bronzed men would appear and load the drugs onto the boats. Then the lights would vanish, bound for Cuba and ports on the East Coast of the United States.

▼ ▼ ▼

Santiago moved into the Fernández condominium, on the beach. The El Rodadero tourist season was coming to a close, and the population had begun to thin out. Only those few proprietors who lived in the town year-round were keeping their stores and shops open. A half-dozen Hell's Angels, their bodies as tanned as baked hams, spent the days playing ball on the beach; their slender girlfriends, followed by attack dogs, walked through the sand in spike heels and tiny bikinis. Several older couples still lounged in the sun, and local young-sters lolled around smoking Santa Marta Gold and Sierra hash.

Mario explained that this scenic part of the country lived in terror of vendettas. Two factions of the Mafia were at work and at war, "The 'white Mafia,'" said Mario, "is you and me and people like us. And the 'black Mafia'—it's those ugly Goajiro monkeys horning in on the marijuana trade." The Goajiros were known to fi-nance subversives, and it was from Cuban ports that, with the blessing of Fidel Castro, their drug shipments were smuggled into the States. Feuds between Goajiro factions were extraordinarily savage.

One afternoon in Santa Marta, Santiago saw the Goa-jiros in action. He was skimming a magazine at a café when a jeep screeched to a halt. Two short, shiny Goa-jiros in skin-tight emerald green and scarlet jumpsuits got out, raced through the restaurant brandishing mag-num revolvers, and opened fire on a young man who sat drinking a few feet from Santiago. The shower of bullets was short and noisy; no one moved or spoke until the jeep tore away. Santiago left hurriedly before the police arrived.

Upset, he told Mario that he wanted to return to Bogotá. "Oh man, please. If you can't handle a little street action, go back to New England. Besides, I promised Antonio I'd take you to the farm."

6 ▽

The Sierra Nevada—one of the highest mountains in the Americas, where the Andes range ends after running the length of South America from Patagonia to Colombia—is less than an hour from El Rodadero by highway and only a few minutes by plane. The valleys are extremely fertile, rich in crystalline rills descending from the perpetual mountain snow; at the beginning of the century, this land was used for banana farming.

At the two-thousand-foot level of the Sierra is a viper-infested jungle. In its heart the Tairona culture once flourished; the work of Tairona goldsmiths was so well known that Incan and Aztec craftsmen traveled to the Sierra to learn the art of gold sculpture. Nearby lived cannibalistic Caribbean nomads, who preyed on Spanish mercenaries traveling though the area in search of El Dorado.

▼ ▼ ▼

Mario and Santiago left at five in the morning. The driver barreled the jeep up a narrow road, seemingly oblivious to the farmers on horseback and mules loaded with fruit that were coming the other way. As they climbed, the vegetation became greener and thicker and the plants grew larger. Banana farms, then coffee plantations, flashed by. They sped past huts, cabins, pastures, roadstands, and towns abuzz with activity. The road grew more primitive. After two hours the wooden bridges were barely as wide as the car; under them ran rapid, clear streams over enormous rocks.

As they climbed into the mountains the air became more humid. Wild orchids hung from the branches of tall, leafy trees. Peacocks and pheasants, their long tails abundant and golden, flew among the thick branches, and hummingbirds cut the peaceful air like resplendent darts. In this region some of the butterflies were yellow with black stripes or sleeves; others were indigo blue, as if they had peeled off the opaline skin of the sea.

A mosslike grass had overgrown the highway's final stretch. In the distance, above the treetops, loomed the snowy peaks of the Sierra Nevada. The jeep rolled over the grass and into a small clearing, where a helicopter was waiting. Santiago and Mario said goodbye to the driver and, accompanied by Mario's two bodyguards, climbed on board.

They headed northeast, over an emerald sea of trees. After an hour, Mario signaled the pilot to hover. "Look," he shouted to Santiago above the roar. "That's one of the lost cities of the Taironas."

Santiago could see nothing through the jungle. Then he thought he made out a ring of dark rock circling a small hill. The pilot brought the helicopter so low that the treetops shivered, but the jungle revealed nothing more.

"It's impossible to see the ruins from up here," Mario yelled. "The jungle buried them long ago. That's why they weren't discovered earlier. Now they're overgrown with marijuana."

The helicopter picked up altitude and continued its monotonous route over the dense woods.

Santiago's interest had been piqued. "I didn't know that these ruins existed," he shouted back.

Mario drew Santiago closer and spoke in his ear. "The peasants have always known about them. For hundreds of years, they've been digging like dogs for gold in the tombs. The problem with the ruins is that they're on marijuana land, and the landowners don't care about anything but their weed. You'll see, we'll visit one of them."

Half an hour later they landed on a small strip cut into the middle of the jungle. Three hundred yards from the runway was an old two-story wooden house. "This plan-tation, *Río Frío*, belonged to your father," Mario said.

While Mario organized the outing to the ruins, San-tiago met the servants and strolled around the grounds. A vodka-clear river, its strong current stroking a white sand riverbed, crossed a small banana grove. Yucca and coffee plants camouflaged a marijuana crop.

Santiago sat under a mango tree to escape the sun.

"*Río Frío*," he said aloud. He remembered the place dimly. He realized with a start that this was the house he had lived in with his mother when he was small. He remembered the humid, sticky heat. He remembered his fear of snakes—sitting all night on his chair with a candle burning waiting for the dawn.

A little after three in the afternoon, Santiago and Mario, with two guards and a farm worker, started out on horseback. The rocky path was narrow; the tropical vegetation was luxurious and exuberant. Everything was so silent that Santiago felt he and his friend were bound for a forbidden place.

The jungle seemed to vibrate with every step, and flowers seemed to bloom before their eyes. After they rode for an hour, the path came to an end on a mossy terrace, beneath which tumultuous streams were hurrying toward the valley. The blue sky opened above them. They dismounted and tied the horses to low tree branches.

Mario pointed to a green wall of vegetation and said, "There's the shortcut. Every time we go to the ruins we open it with machetes, but by the next day it has always grown back." He looked at his friend. "Whatever happens, Santiago," he said, "don't lose sight of me. If you fall behind, forget it. I know people who have disappeared, eaten by the jungle." He paused and grinned.

Santiago, wished he was back at the house, resting in a hammock on a breezy balcony drinking a *Cuba Libre*.

The worker hacked at the jungle with his machete; Santiago, Mario, and the guards followed at a short distance. As they advanced, continuous, repetitious sounds spread through the forest and created an echo like the prolonged roll of a thunderclap in the heavy air. Forty-five minutes later, sweating and *savia*-stained, they reached a hilltop clearing.

"This is where the ruins start," Mario announced.

Santiago's eyes followed his friend's gaze. Before them dangled a curtain of vines, giving no clue to what lay beyond. They pushed through and found a rocky path overgrown with milk-colored moss. Heavy ferns swung on both sides. Santiago jumped, thinking he'd seen a snake slide like lightning over some palm leaves. He paused and discovered that it was just sunlight.

Finally, they found themselves on a stone platform, beside an obelisk three yards high. Mario explained that beneath them were the ruins of an ancient sacrificial temple; the sea of dry leaves the men were walking on had been accumulating for centuries. A stale humid odor like dried blood pervaded the air. The rocks on the inside of the altar were sparkling white. Visible in the area around the altar were four small hills connected by a system of staircases and notched by rock terraces. On each hill stood a temple.

Santiago sat down on the ruins. Exhausted and limping badly, Mario came to his side. "It's really a workout for me to come here," he said. "I'm not very good at these jaunts, but if it weren't for experiences like this, life wouldn't be worth a damn. Ruins are important to me." He sat down next to Santiago; he was sweating and his face was red. "This whole area is covered with temples and tombs and terraces. The Taironas worked primarily with gold, but also clay. *Guaqueros,* in search of gold, have destroyed most of the ceramics. Your father-in-law has tried to stop the gravediggers. But this jungle is so dense that even an army couldn't do much good."

"How strange," said Santiago.

Mario stood up and smiled. "I want to visit two temples I've never seen. They're nearby. Want to come?"

Santiago wanted to soak in this place's atmosphere. He told Mario he would rather rest up for the return hike.

"Catch you later," Mario called as he and his party

left. "Don't get any ideas and start wandering around. *Ciao.*"

A few minutes later all traces of the group had disappeared, as if enfolded in a green shroud. Santiago let his eyes roam over the jungle. Monkeys played in the branches of trees, their yells and shrieks echoing in the distance. Iridescent toucans perched on ruins only a few yards away. A tangle of clear streams flowed down the hills, remnants of what had obviously once been an intricate irrigation system.

Parakeets and parrots nested in mango, *mamey,* and fig trees. Santiago looked up; two squawking macaws sailed through the sky. Like fragments of a rainbow, he thought.

Moved by this vision, he got up to explore the rest of the ruins, turned, and saw a thin green snake. It paused, eyed him, and slithered away down some stairs. Santiago let out his breath, felt his heart pound, and recalled his first encounter with a snake. It was when he was six. His father had taken him on a hunting expedition. When the dogs picked up a scent, he ordered Santiago to sit down under a tree and crossed a stream in search of tracks. Santiago was still watching the place where his father had disappeared when a serpent slid up to him. Santiago sat perfectly still. Neither he nor the snake stirred until almost nightfall. Then a shot rang out and the snake flew through the air in pieces. Santiago looked around. His father, on the other bank, was on his knees cleaning the gun. Santiago began to cry. When his father reached him he told the boy, "Men don't cry. Pick up the pieces. It's meat for the dogs." Santiago recalled gathering the pieces of snake, and how they writhed in his hands.

Recovering his composure, he went to inspect the interior of the temple. Dusk was deepening. He felt strangely calm. As he moved deeper into the dark, he understood that the uninviting valley below, the long stretches of marijuana, and the ruins with their tombs full of gold were also a part of what he was.

7 ▽

Before they went to bed that night, Mario told Santiago that they were in luck—it was "the night of the fireflies." The marijuana plants known as Santa Marta Gold, after being fertilized for months with sugar dissolved in water, reached such a degree of potency that, once a year, their leaves shone in the dark. "It's worth seeing," Mario advised. "Set your alarm for three."

Although he was emotionally and physically exhausted, Santiago slept fitfully. After midnight, he woke with a start, disoriented, struggling to remember where he was. A memory came back to him. Villalba's old gamekeeper came to the house holding in one hand several bloody severed fingers. Villalba reprimanded him for the mess and for his carelessness, shoved a fifty-peso bill into one bloody palm, and fired him on the spot.

The weight of this memory left him wide awake, staring into the darkness. Santiago rose and went into Mario's room. Through the mosquito net he saw his friend's naked body. Mario was snoring loudly. Santiago lifted the net and tapped him on the shoulder; Mario rolled over and continued snoring. Santiago studied the pointed stump of Mario's leg. He realized he wanted to fondle and lick it. He returned to his own room, poured some cognac from the bottle on the night table, and lay back down, hoping to sleep. He had dozed off when, through his dreams, he heard a weak dull murmur echoing like ominous music. The buzzing faded and returned, faded and returned, again and again; Santiago felt as if he were rolling on waves.

Something pricked his ears, then his neck, cheeks, arms, and legs. He slapped and rubbed his body with his open palms. He felt better. When he closed his eyes again, the buzzing returned, and was followed by abrupt silence.

Santiago woke fully and reached out from under the mosquito net to turn on the light. Thousands of mosquitoes, like a shower of pepper, swarmed past his arm and into the net. He withdrew his arm. The sound returned and rose in a crescendo. Mosquitoes gathered around the light, obscuring it and creating a grotesque cloud.

The white of the netting darkened, as if being tinged with soot. An irrational fear began to take hold of Santiago. Suddenly, his self-control snapped. He thrashed about under the net, clapping the air wildly, smacking his body. With every blow, he killed dozens of mosquitoes. His hands were smeared with blackish fetid blood.

Tearing the net aside, he rushed toward the bathroom, but stopped in his tracks at the window. Outside, bright-red flashes were twinkling; the tropical night seemed an ethereal Christmas tree. So this is the night of the fireflies, he thought. The beauty of the sight left Santiago breathless. He sat down on the windowsill and inhaled deeply. The murmur of the streams and rivers that converged near the house drowned the angry buzzing of the mosquitoes. Diamondlike stars hung in a velvety sky. Santiago was regaining his composure when the mosquitoes gathered around him, then flew out the window.

Minutes later he understood why. Fat heavy drops of water hit nearby leaves. Behind this splattering rose a huge sound, like a rising tide. It was a thunderstorm. The marijuana leaves lost their glow. The rain fell in sheets and lightning sketched electric patterns in the sky. The sound of the falling rain anesthetized Santiago. He returned to bed and fell asleep.

When he awoke at dawn to the crowing of roosters, his eyes were heavy, as if filled with sand. On the first floor, servants were already bustling. Outside, in the already-dry fields, burros were clopping and cows were lowing softly. The pale dawn seemed soothing.

At six o'clock, he got up and showered, letting the cold water run over his swollen, mosquito-bitten body. After dressing, he went down to sit on the terrace. Crisp air that had drifted down from the regions of perpetual snow was mingling with the warm odor of cow manure. He savored a cup of coffee, brought by the cook, until Mario appeared. The two bodyguards, still half asleep, staggered along behind him.

"Jesus. Were you feeding the mosquitoes last night?" was Mario's greeting. His eyes danced. "Let's go, man. *¡Pilas!*"

Santiago wondered if his friend had been snorting coke before breakfast.

"I mean, *gringo,* let's get out of here before it gets hot."

They went aloft again in the helicopter. The peaks of the Sierra Nevada dominated the landscape. Marijuana plantations extended for hundreds of miles and were crossed by dirt roads and landing fields, some of them tiny, others big enough for Lear jets. Mario pointed out gangs of men setting fields ablaze and miles of rugged terrain already razed by fire.

"For the sake of propaganda, we have to burn part of the harvest," Mario explained. "The Colombian and American governments then release photographs of black stubble celebrating their 'war' on the drug trade, you dig it?" Mario threw back his head and laughed.

Towns had sprung up all over the area. They appeared to be inhabited almost entirely by children. The workers had guns and drove their jeeps and trucks at top speed, raising whirlwinds of dust on the open roads. In the larger villages, Mario told Santiago, there were brothels full of women who came from the cities to work as prostitutes to support their families.

He continued talking over the noise of the helicopter. Drugs, alcohol, and a primitive kind of machismo were pervasive, he said, and violence was the norm. Men killed at the slightest provocation; for a few thousand pesos or a few grams of cocaine, contract killers could be hired to do away with anyone. Murders were committed over women and bets, and out of sheer braggadocio. "That's our beautiful Colombia," he said mockingly.

As they crossed over dense jungle, Mario said, "Fernández needs your help. You can't just unload your land; who are you going to sell it to? The white Mafia already have enough problems with what they've got. Sell the business to the Goajiro chiefs? Forget it. Sure, they've got the money to buy, but they're fucking savages who came out of the desert a few years ago. We can't even deal with them, let alone trust them."

The helicopter broke through a cloud and emerged over the ocean, which was tinted crimson by the sunset. Santiago leaned out of the window; in the distance the Sierra Nevada gleamed like a strawberry cone.

"Gold-rush country, Santiago. You're looking at it," Mario said. He rummaged in his pocket and gave a pipe to one of his bodyguards. The man cleaned, stuffed, and lit it, filling the helicopter with fragrant smoke as Mario talked. "We have to take advantage of the situation while we can. This place is incredible—first gold, then bananas, now grass. Who knows what it'll be next? Oil? Things change, man. Ten years ago, no one was growing dope—there was no competition. But now . . ."

Fernández's line, thought Santiago.

When the helicopter landed, night had begun to fall and the evening breeze was blowing up from the sea. Mario's driver greeted them with the news that Beatrice had arrived from New York the day before and was waiting for Santiago at the El Rodadero apartment.

Beatrice's room was dark and the curtains were drawn when Santiago arrived. He approached the bed; he could hear his wife's light breathing. He remembered the night he had met Beatrice. Because of her plastic surgery, he had seldom been able to see her in daylight, and she had always seemed a creature of the shadows. Santiago hesitated: Should he leave the room or sit down on the bed and wake her? Then he saw that her eyes were open. She was smiling in the darkness.

"I have a surprise for you, my dear. You're going to be a father," she said.

Santiago lit the lamp and took Beatrice in his arms. She was wearing a pink negligee; a smile of a kind he'd never seen was on her lips. Her usually drawn face had already begun to fill out.

"Why didn't you tell me before?" he asked.

"I didn't want to worry you. I wanted to wait until the doctors said the baby was out of danger."

"Wouldn't it be safer to have the baby in New York?"

Taking Santiago's hand and placing it on her stomach, Beatrice explained to him that a special nurse would be arriving momentarily and that a month before the baby was due the doctor would come to be with her. "I wanted to have it here and nowhere else," she said. Beatrice's green eyes grew misty. "I didn't tell you because I thought I'd miscarry again. I wanted to be sure. Nobody knew—not my friends in New York, not even my parents." She sighed. "I should rest now. The doctor told me not to get too excited." She lay back on the pillow, her long blond hair reaching to her swollen breasts. Santiago turned off the light and waited until he heard her breathing steadily; then he took her hand in his and caressed it.

Antonio and Graciela came to stay at the El Rodadero apartment. Fernández, who had never had a son, was drunk with happiness; for the first time in years, he was affectionate toward Santiago and had the good sense not to mention the family business. In his enthusiasm, he notified the major newspapers of the impending birth and scheduled a celebratory Mass in Santa Marta Cathedral for the first Sunday in March.

The country's most prominent families were invited. Caught up in the excitement, Santiago busied himself with plans, and realized a week before the Mass that he was happy. Several guests arrived early, to enjoy the empty beach. The only guest of consequence unable to come was the President, who sent his regrets at the last minute.

The morning of the Mass, the ocean was rough and gray and heavy clouds were drizzling. But by ten o'clock the sky was clear and the temperature was soaring as if the most recent rains had fallen days, not hours, earlier.

At noon the procession of limousines pulled to a stop in front of the cathedral. Santiago, Beatrice, and her family stepped out of their Mercedes and flashbulbs went off around them. Any cooling breeze must be confined to a far corner of the world, thought Santiago.

Beatrice took him by the arm, and they walked a few steps behind her parents up the steps covered in red velvet and down the aisle to their seats. Aglow with happiness, she wore a sleeveless white organdy dress. The low neck revealed her perfect shoulders and bosom. Her hair hung loose, and her lips were painted bright Aztec pink.

The heat inside the high-ceilinged church was intense. Santiago took off his white suit jacket, folded it over his knees, and loosened his tie. The cathedral was full but silent; only the crackling of the candles on the altar could be heard. Beatrice received communion at the end of the Mass. As the white-clad body, flanked by rows of candles, knelt on the damask cushion, Santiago found himself moved.

After the Mass, though the bodyguards cleared a path through the crowd, it still took an interminable twenty minutes to reach the cathedral door. Outside, the noon sun was oppressive; even the people protected by hats and parasols or by the almond trees were perspiring profusely.

The Fernández family stood outside the door accepting congratulations from the guests, waiting for an opportunity to get to the coolness of their cars. The chief of Santa Marta's police was paying his respects to Beatrice when a thickset Goajiro fired a revolver. The bullets punctured each of the police chief's eyes, Mafia style. His body collapsed against Beatrice, who fell to the ground.

More shots were fired and the crowd became a stampede of screaming, dodging bodies. The bodyguards formed a semicircle around the family and Antonio and Graciela scurried to the car. Santiago had swept Beatrice up and was placing her in the back seat when a wounded man clutched at her leg. A bodyguard reached out and fired a shot through the man's mouth; whitish clumps of brain landed several feet away. Santiago jumped in. As the car began to move, the back door—still open—slapped at the crowd, and Beatrice let out a scream. It was then that Santiago saw blood spurting like a geyser from a bullet wound in her stomach. He yelled to the chauffeur to take them to the hospital. Beatrice's face contorted in agony.

The car flew through the streets of Santa Marta and braked to a halt in front of the hospital's emergency entrance. Santiago, with Beatrice in his arms, ran through the hallways, leaving a trail of blood. No doctors were on duty; it was Sunday afternoon. Nurses hooked up the blood-transfusion unit and tried to locate a surgeon. Several physicians had been at the Mass, but no one except the family knew how badly Beatrice had been hurt. Her breathing was becoming erratic.

Almost half an hour had passed when Mario Simán ran into the emergency room with Dr. Martínez in tow. The doctor looked at Beatrice and said there wasn't a moment to lose—they'd have to operate.

By the time the operation was under way, television and newspaper reporters had stationed themselves in the hospital corridor. Inquisitive faces and blinding flashes of light appeared every time a nurse opened the waiting-room door. Fernández ordered the bodyguards to clear the reporters out.

Two hours later, Dr. Martínez emerged from the operating room, exhausted. He lowered his head. "We did what we could," he said in a strained voice. "But we couldn't save the child. All we can do now is pray for Beatrice."

Beatrice was moved to intensive care. Mario offered his jet to fly her to New York to see her doctors, but Martínez said she should not be moved. With martyred resignation Graciela sat at her daughter's side, rosary in hand; Antonio cursed and paced.

As night began to fall, Santiago, holding Beatrice's hand, saw her open her eyes. They were full of both sadness and joy. Sadness, Santiago knew, at the loss of her child; relief, he guessed, at leaving a world where she had suffered so much. She opened her mouth and raised her hand first to her breasts, then to her throat.

The sounds she made were unintelligible to Santiago until he put his ear to her lips. He heard a gurgling and then the words: "The ca-da-ver . . ."

When Santiago lifted his head, Beatrice's eyes had turned into transparent, immobile emeralds. Dr. Martínez came to the bed, took Beatrice's wrist, shook his head, and gently closed her eyelids. Santiago sank into the chair, his gaze adrift in the dark. All he could hear was the monotonous hum of the air conditioner.

The next day Beatrice's body was flown by helicopter to Barranquilla for the funeral. The newspapers covered the death on their front pages; hundreds of people appeared at the cathedral and the cemetery. As the sun slipped behind the horizon, the coffin was lowered into an open grave near Alvaro Villalba's plot. Santiago, heavily sedated, was already convinced that Beatrice's death —and the death of his unborn child—was his punishment for patricide.

8 ▽

Santiago returned to Bogotá as the city's brief summer ended and the rainy season began. Unlike the storms of the tropics, which are sporadic, the rain in Bogotá falls almost continuously. Mist descends, uncontainable, from the mountains, and a dense, cottony carpet stations itself overhead, opening before the pale sun for only a few minutes as night falls. Even in homes with central heating, a chill creeps in under doors and through cracks in windows, poisoning everything.

Distraught, guilt-ridden, Santiago knew he had to make certain decisions about his life. He considered pursuing a career, but felt incapable of doing so. He ignored Fernández's calls. Submerged in his despair, he turned to drugs and was soon spending most of his days snorting Mario's unending supply of cocaine. He stopped eating regular meals; unable to sleep, he began to rely on barbiturates.

Meanwhile he welcomed any diversion that might distract him. He would go across town to the red-light district and buy the services of attractive prostitutes; once they were in bed, he would lose all interest in sex. He didn't know whether to blame his impotence on the cocaine or the sordidness of the rooms he was taken to, places where he was afraid of being robbed, hurt, or infected with an incurable venereal disease.

His attention shifted to Blanca. He had fired the old couple who had worked for his father and hired her, a beautiful fifteen-year-old girl with shiny black hair, oriental eyes, and skin the color of brown *panela* sugar. From the first she seemed to know that something was wrong with her employer. She avoided him and, whenever they crossed paths, eyed him suspiciously. Though the girl was probably still a virgin, his thoughts dwelled on her, and he became obsessed with the idea of sleeping with her. He studied her movements and prowled the halls surreptitiously, following her.

One night, as he was watching the evening news, the picture on the screen went blank and the newscaster's voice cut off. Santiago had gotten up to fiddle with the set when the image cleared. An intense young woman with short hair, dark glasses, and a straw hat obscuring most of her forehead dominated the screen.

"Comrades," she shouted, "the February 1969 movement—to counteract the new wave of torture unleashed by military thugs aided by Yankee imperialism—is striking a blow at the Colombian government." The woman thrust a sword at the camera and waved it. "This sword belonged to the great liberator Simón Bolívar. We have taken it from the National Museum. This symbol of our liberty will not be returned until the Colombian people are free. Long live our brothers, fallen in the struggle. Long live F-69!"

The image flickered, and the newscaster, who moments before had been reading an international press release, reappeared. Behind his desk, he sat yelling, "*¿Qué pasa? ¿Qué pasa?*"

Santiago flicked the dial. What had happened? Where had that woman come from? What was F-69? He tried to call Mario, then Caridad; neither was in.

The news about F-69's broadcast appeared on the front page of the morning papers. One newspaper reproduced the young woman's proclamation, and described F-69 as a "terrorist movement dedicated to the destruction of law and order, and to the so-called liberation of the Colombian nation." The young woman was identified as twenty-four-year-old Policarpa Samper, the daughter of one of the country's oldest families. The article was accompanied by photos of the girl and her parents from the 1970s when she had run away from her convent school. Other stories focused on the robbery of Bolívar's sword from the National Museum.

As he walked to the Hotel Guatavita that afternoon to buy foreign periodicals, Santiago noticed that most people were walking hurriedly and speaking in whispers. Panic seemed painted on their faces. Army troops, usually appearing only at night, marched through the *avenidas* behind heavy tanks, like strange extraterrestrial invaders.

On the six-o'clock news, General Juan Raúl Roca promised the Colombian people that he would find and crush the subversives.

▼ ▼ ▼

After breakfast the next day, Santiago went out onto the terrace. It was ten o'clock, but the heavy rain made it seem like twilight. He leaned on the railing, looked down, and saw that all the cars in the streets had heavy branches tied to their fenders. Puzzled by the strange sight, he went into the kitchen. Blanca was washing dishes and listening to salsa music. She wore sandals; Santiago silently admired her pretty feet and her shapely tawny legs for a moment before speaking.

"Please, could you turn that down a little?" he asked.

She went to the radio and switched it off.

Santiago was disconcerted. "No, no, don't turn it off. It's just that it was too loud."

"I play it because of the news, Don Santiago," she said meekly, averting her eyes when they met his as if she were guilty of some crime.

"Tell me, do you know the meaning of the branches tied to the buses and cars?"

Blanca tried to stifle a smile. "To sweep away the tacks and nails," she said confidently. "When people get mad, they talk about burning things and going on strike, but mostly they spill nails on the streets."

"Who is mad?"

"People in the barrio." She gestured vaguely with her hand. "Things are expensive, and if you don't have money for the bus, how you going to find work?"

Santiago was uncomfortable with the turn the conversation was taking. He also was aware that this girl was the only contact he had had with the outside world since Beatrice's death. The other two people he knew in Bogotá, Caridad and Mario, he had not seen since his return from El Rodadero. "I'm going to rest for a while," he announced. "I'm not very hungry, so don't call me for lunch."

"Sí, señor, Don Santiago," she said, once again avoiding his eyes.

He left the kitchen, closing the door behind him, and the salsa music rose from the radio. From his bedroom window, he looked at Monserrate. It was completely wrapped in fog; only the steeple was visible above the mist.

He tried to nap but tossed and turned instead. Images of Caridad and Blanca crossed his mind, and he masturbated. He got up and paced the room, feeling like a prisoner in his own penthouse.

Maybe I should close the apartment and return to New York, he thought. Now that Beatrice was dead, he felt as if the anchor that had kept him tied to reality all these years had been lifted. Too miserable to go out, he had Blanca serve him dinner in his room and watched television until a voice announced the end of broadcasting for the day. The screen went blank to the strains of the national anthem. Santiago turned off the set and got ready for bed.

Clutching a pillow, he closed his eyes and tried to force himself to dream. An hour later he was still awake. He fought the urge to take more barbiturates; he got up, poured himself a cognac, and wandered out onto the terrace.

The night was humid but the rain had stopped. The streets glowed brightly under the streetlights, but only a few cars passed by. An old man in a black *ruana* appeared on the street below, leading a rickety donkey loaded with garbage cans; the man walked hunched over, as if his will had been broken. A dog barked in the distance. A shot rang out, and a scream followed it.

Nighttime in the big city, Santiago thought. He returned to the living room and turned on the stereo. Only one station—a rock music station—was broadcasting. He took a silver box from behind the bookcase and spent a half hour snorting cocaine. His brain began to buzz and his body felt electric.

He put the cocaine away and crossed the apartment to the servant's wing. There were doors on each side of the corridor; Santiago wasn't sure which led to Blanca's room. He opened one. When his eyes adjusted to the dark, he made out a body on the small bed. It was Blanca. One leg peeked out from under the blanket. Santiago walked to her, knelt down, and began to caress her thigh. She rolled over without waking up. He put his hand under the covers and placed it on her belly. Enjoying the warmth, he started to pull off her panties. She awoke. "What is it? What's going on? Who's there?" she cried.

"It's me, Blanca, Don Santiago." He spoke quietly and evenly and did not remove his hand. The girl sat up; Santiago pushed her back down. She screamed, and Santiago clapped his hand over her mouth. Her eyes bulged in fright, their pupils expanding in the dim light. She bit down hard on the flesh of Santiago's palm. "You little cannibal," he said. He grabbed the pillow, pushed it into her face, and rolled on top of her.

"Calm down," he murmured. "I'm not going to hurt you. Calm down."

Santiago used his free hand to pull down her panties. The girl writhed, and scratched his back again and again, but he pried her thighs open and, with one thrust, penetrated her. He moaned in pleasure as a torrent of semen flowed from his penis. He removed the pillow. Blanca lay still but breathing. Santiago got up and walked out of the room, closing the door behind him.

When he fell asleep that night, Santiago had a dream he had had before once. In the dream, he tried unsuccessfully to rouse himself from a nervous sleep as dawn light filtered through the curtains. He attempted to open his eyes and they wouldn't obey; he wanted to roll over but his body was paralyzed.

Then the dream took a new twist; it began to bleed into his actual state. Soon he felt genuinely incapable of rising out of sleep. This can't really be happening, he thought. It's just my imagination playing tricks. If I stay still for a minute and count to sixty, everything will return to normal. He counted the seconds slowly and at sixty tried to open his eyes. He couldn't. He could feel the sun warming the room, but he couldn't see it. His heart seemed to be beating but he didn't seem to be breathing. Was this death? It can't be, he thought. If it were, I'd be rigid and cold. Besides, I can hear noise: Blanca vacuuming the apartment, traffic on the street. The heat grew more intense. His face and neck itched, but he couldn't move his hands to scratch. Maybe I am dead. Maybe I'm already dead and no one knows it, he thought. He tried to scream, but his lips wouldn't open and a howl lodged behind his clenched teeth. Then he felt sweat trickle down his palms and tears well up behind his eyelids. He was alive. The relief was momentary. If he didn't get up soon, Blanca might come in and, no doubt with pleasure, think he was dead. His fear began to edge into panic. She'd call the doctor, who'd come and sign the death certificate. At the funeral, nobody would suspect he was alive. He imagined himself deposited in the tomb, near his father's and Beatrice's bodies, alive but unable to tell anyone. His fear took an unfamiliar turn. Maybe this is what death is, he mused. When one dies, the soul does not abandon the body but is kept prisoner by it. Maybe the soul decomposes as the body does; maybe it has its own worms. If the soul, like the body, is finally devoured, then death isn't so horrible, because there's no possibility of eternal punishment.

As a feeling of peace at the idea of an eternal void flooded him, the telephone rang and jolted him out of his dream. His eyes popped open, and he heard Blanca say that she would tell Don Santiago that he was invited to dinner at Mario Simán's that night.

Santiago spent most of the day in bed, overcome with lassitude. He had not expected to feel remorse. He knew very well that, in Colombia, young maids are routinely used by the master of the house or his children; he knew that Blanca had grown up expecting this to be her fate; he also knew that had she been working elsewhere, sooner or later she would have been sexually abused. Yet this knowledge did not exonerate him. He suspected that even if she wanted to quit she couldn't afford to give up the job that supported her parents. The few times they passed one another, she drew away from him and avoided his gaze.

At six that evening, Santiago fled the apartment and walked the few blocks to Mario's. In the living room, in front of the fireplace, Mario and Caridad sat listening to music. As the three friends exchanged pleasantries, Santiago couldn't keep his eyes off Caridad; he hadn't seen her since the night of their first meeting a little more than a month earlier. She had since cut her hair into a short bob that emphasized the arrogance of her features. She wore no jewelry and seemed preoccupied. Her makeup was blotchy and her eyes were red, as if she had been crying all day.

Santiago sipped a drink and rehearsed his words. "I've been thinking of leaving Colombia and going back to New York," he said.

His two friends looked at him sharply, but neither spoke. Caridad broke the silence, hissing: "Do you have any idea what's happened?"

Santiago was taken aback. "Apparently not."

Caridad let out a laugh that was triumphant and sarcastic, and said to Mario, "You see?"

A feeling of guilt took hold of Santiago; now he understood why Caridad had been chosen to head PAX.

"Cool it," Mario said. "Don't get nasty. Santiago isn't responsible for what Fernández does, and you know it."

Santiago looked from one to the other in confusion. "What has my father-in-law done?" he asked.

Caridad stood up and walked to the bar to pour herself a drink. "You tell him," she said to Mario.

"Your father-in-law has started one of the worst vendettas in the history of Colombia. He has conveniently used Beatrice's death as an excuse to declare war on the black Mafia."

"But Beatrice's death was an accident," Santiago said to Mario. He was afraid to confront Caridad, who with her short hair and stark look seemed more beautiful and cruel than ever.

"Accidental, my foot," Caridad said. "In this country very little is accidental."

"So what did Antonio do?" Santiago asked. He suspected he wouldn't like the answer.

"The government has kept the press gagged on this," Mario explained. "But your father-in-law had the Villanueva family rubbed out. Only one son—at school in the States—escaped. So you get the picture, let me tell you how Fernández did it. He had bombs set off in their homes on the Atlantic Coast and in Miami. Then he ordered his men to chop up all the relatives, children, and wives of the *cacique* and sprinkle them through downtown Miami at rush hour. That's your father-in-law."

Santiago shivered; he sipped his drink and his eyes wandered from Caridad to Mario and around the room. How strange that Beatrice's death should bring about such a horror, he thought. She was so gentle and innocent—a child, really.

"And now for the big surprise. The Goajiros have vowed to get their revenge by toppling the government," Mario continued. "They just signed a pact with the guerrillas. The army is furious; General Juan Raúl Roca has threatened a coup of his own if the government doesn't get its shit together fast."

"PAX can't control everything," Caridad said bitterly. "Juan Raúl is right."

"Would my leaving help?" Santiago asked.

His friends burst out laughing.

Caridad planted herself in front of him. "Work with us instead," she said. "The government has just created a new bureau—the Ministry of Public Information. I'm sure Mario's father would name you minister. You look good, and you've lived in the States, so you must understand television."

"Me a minister? You must be kidding," said Santiago. But he was intrigued. "What kind of minister?"

"The ministry's just an extension of the armed forces," Mario explained. "They want a civilian as head in order to keep the public happy, and we think you'll do. You'll learn how to run the country. Let's face it once and for all: It's a good way to protect our interests. Every day, it becomes more and more obvious that the Cubans and the Goajiros are working together. And the Goajiro *caciques* want to wipe out the old aristocracy, better known as thee and me."

"But what would I do? What does the ministry do?" Santiago asked.

"It's in charge of handling the media," Caridad said. "PAX can't do it alone. But you won't have to take anyone on personally, and you'll have the army's full cooperation."

"And as long as things are cool, the generals are happy," said Mario. "Remember, though, if the government doesn't pull it together fast there could be a coup any day."

Caridad smiled. "But you don't have to make up your mind tonight. You have until . . . tomorrow," she said, laughing.

This spiel of theirs sounds rehearsed, thought Santiago.

"Hey, man, don't look so serious. You've lucked out. Tomorrow afternoon we'll go see my father and send an official announcement to the press."

"Well, I'll think about it," Santiago said.

Caridad stood up. "Let's do some coke," she said to Mario, smoothing her hair.

He pointed to a bookcase. She took the gold disc, tapped a pyramid of white powder on it, and held it to Santiago's nostrils; he inhaled deeply. He didn't know which excited him more—the cocaine or the contact with Caridad's black fingernail. He took her hand and kissed it. Caridad kneeled on the rug and pulled him toward her.

"Trust me," she crooned. "I know what's good for you."

9 ▽

The Presidential Palace—on the Carrera Séptima in the colonial section of Bogotá—is surrounded by the Capitol, the Planetarium, the Ministry of Mines, the Temple of San Augustín, and the Arts and Crafts Museum. Mario's chauffeur guided the limousine along the yellow road. Santiago gazed through the windows at gardens of geraniums, *romeros,* Arabian jasmine, *albahaca,* fuchsias, and Jericho roses; Mario explained that the palace had been constructed in the middle of the eighteenth century as the home of Antonio Nariño, a wealthy young aristocrat known in Colombian history as *El Precursor* because he had translated the Rights of Man from French into Spanish. The translation was not appreciated, and it brought about Nariño's eventual incarceration and premature death.

The car stopped in front of the palace doors. A dozen heavily armed young guards, dressed in green, red, and cadmium yellow uniforms, looked on. To the right of the entrance was a ten-foot-high pre-Columbian stone statue, and on the left a modern red metal sculpture. Before he entered, Santiago turned and looked up: The rainy afternoon sky was the color of ash.

They were received by the Chief of Protocol. Mario had him take Santiago on a tour of the lower floor of the building and went to the kitchen for a snack. A great deal of light flooded the palace, but the silence was sepulchral. Every room boasted enormous solemn paintings of different events in Colombia's struggle for independence. Security guards were everywhere, hidden behind white pillars; from time to time, a servant glided by.

The Chief of Protocol opened a high white door. "The meeting room for the Council of Ministers," he announced, and gestured to a long wide *guayacán* table; Mario was already there. The room was simple and modern. The walls were painted white; behind the presidential chair hung the Colombian shield. It was a national joke that one of the shield's most prominent elements—the Isthmus of Panama—no longer belonged to Colombia, and that another, the condor, was almost extinct.

As Santiago leaned forward to ask Mario when the President was expected, the door opened and a maid, her face bearing smallpox scars, entered, carrying a silver coffee service. They poured themselves two steaming, aromatic cups, and looked up when the door opened again. The President, a bovine sixty-year-old man, moving as if afflicted with arthritis, tottered through it.

Mario stood up and kissed his father on the cheek. When Santiago held out his hand, the President, instead of shaking it, caught him around the shoulder and squeezed his arm; Santiago found the gesture reassuring. They sat down. Simán smiled affectionately at his son, took his hand, and looked at Santiago.

"I see you already have coffee," he said. "Imagine how it feels to see you sitting here, Santiago. You're the spitting image of your father. He was already a grown man when I met him, but I know he had your face in his youth."

Santiago felt a fleeting shock; it had never occurred to him that he bore any resemblance to Villalba. The President went on, "I'm pleased that you—" He stopped, as if he had forgotten what he was saying, and gestured helplessly with his hands.

"Papa, are you all right? Would you like some coffee?" asked Mario.

The President shook his head and his face came to life again. "Yes, thank you, son." Taking the cup, he turned to Santiago. "By the end of the day, I'm exhausted. If the people knew how hard I work they wouldn't sympathize with the terrorists." He inhaled the steam from his cup. "It's a shame we don't have more people like you, Santiago. I'm delighted you've decided to take this ministry post. Your father would be proud of you; you're all Villalba."

Santiago wished the President wouldn't keep referring to his father.

The President spoke in a monotone. "I was telling Mario that I'm glad you two have met again. The only people you can really trust are your friends from childhood—that's what I always say. The others . . ." He raised his eyebrows.

Santiago, casting about for a response, said, "The ministry is an honor. I'm grateful for your confidence. I hope I will not disappoint you."

"You're a young man. You will learn."

"Thank you, thank you very much, *Señor Presidente*."

Mario stood up. "Well, you two have finally met. But now I think we'd better go." He looked at Santiago. "I know you're busy, Papa."

Santiago stood up. The President took his hand, clasped it with some fervor, and said, "Welcome, my young friend. Welcome back to your fatherland."

By the next afternoon the drizzle hadn't stopped. Santiago ran across the sidewalk outside his apartment building and stepped into a black Mercedes; as a member of the government, he now also had a chauffeur at his service.

The Mercedes crossed the National Park and entered the mountains. A dossier open on his lap, Santiago reviewed what he had learned about Stuart G. Hamilton, the U.S. ambassador he'd be meeting. Hamilton, although appointed only last October, had already achieved glory in some circles. Within a mere month of his arrival, he'd engineered an agreement between the U.S. and Colombian governments to fight drug traffic. Soon after, Washington authorized a loan to Colombia for twenty million dollars, dozens of airplanes were shot down, great expanses of marijuana land were burned, and hundreds of people filled the jails on the Atlantic coast. Unrecognizable cadavers, mangled by predatory fish, washed upon the shores of rivers and lakes. The Colombian television networks extolled the campaign, and telegrams of congratulations from the State Department appeared in the international press. Happiest of all with Hamilton's effectiveness were the aristocratic landholders; the only cultivators, smugglers, and dealers affected by the new policies had been the Goajiro *caciques* of the black Mafia.

The Mercedes drove past fields full of cows and *lulo* trees, entered a neighborhood of Tudor-style mansions, and pulled to a halt in front of a high wrought-iron gate. Two blond marines, M-16s in hand, checked the papers handed them by the chauffeur and muttered into walkie-talkies. The gate swung open noiselessly. A fine white stone road wound its way through immaculate grounds where a garden of yellow and white roses bloomed. The embassy was a pale blue three-story house in neoclassical style. The terrace, bordered by thick marble columns, was lit by a baroque Murano lamp; its rays reached through the shadowy rain to the garden and gave warmth to the wet rose petals. A doorman carrying an umbrella opened the car door. Breathing in the fresh, eucalyptus-scented mountain air, Santiago crossed the terrace, wiped his shoes on a red rug, and walked inside. An aide introduced himself as Carl Crystal. Santiago held out his hand, and Crystal, with a noticeable American accent, said, *"Por favor, sígame."*

They walked over blue oriental carpets through a marble vestibule and into a large room. Through French doors could be seen an interior garden; a riot of orchids dancing in the rain. Crystal led Santiago to a chair beside the fireplace, told him that the ambassador would arrive shortly, and offered him a drink. Santiago guessed that it wouldn't be appropriate and refused. After the aide left him, Santiago looked around, wondering, Is a hidden camera studying my movements? The ceiling was high, its color contrasting with the intense violet of the walls. He got up and stood before an Albers painting.

It was upside down. He was fighting to repress a chuckle when a voice behind him said, "Welcome, Dr. Villalba." It was Stuart G. Hamilton. They shook hands, and the ambassador, his lips frozen into a smile, led him back to the fireplace. Hamilton was large and plump, but despite his size his gestures were agile, almost youthful. He wore an indigo blue suit.

"I've been looking forward to meeting you," Hamilton said with a Southern accent. "Antonio Fernández is a good friend of mine, and he recommends you as highly as if you were his own son. It's too bad I never got the chance to meet your father. They tell me he was a great man." He paused. "Your appointment to the ministry is good news. We're proud to have you aboard."

Hamilton spoke as if reciting a speech, but in perfect Spanish. Santiago could imagine a situation in which this man with his veneer of civilization might calmly order an execution.

"It's a great honor," Santiago said. "I'm not sure I deserve the distinction."

"Experience makes the man," the ambassador replied. "I learned that in my youth, when I was at West Point. These Latin American countries need men like you— men who have been educated in the States and have an open mind. There are so few of you in this profession." He lowered his voice. "Allow me to express my condolences for the passing of your wife, Beatrice. She was a sweet, lovely woman. I knew her years ago in Washington."

The mention of Beatrice's name put Santiago on edge. Hamilton said quickly, "These terrorists must be exterminated. If I can get rid of them, I'll go to my grave a happy man. Your appointment is a historical event, my dear *amigo*."

Two waiters in livery entered the room with a liquor caddy. The ambassador waved them toward Santiago, who ordered a scotch with mineral water; the ambassador asked for the same. After the waiters disappeared, Hamilton whispered conspiratorially, "In countries like this, you can't trust anybody. You know what I mean."

Santiago nodded, although he wasn't at all sure he did.

"Well, as you all say, *salud!* Or as we *gringos* would have it, cheers." He raised the glass to his lips and drank. "I wanted to tell you that Washington is completely behind you," he went on. "I've spent my whole diplomatic career in South America, and while I know that no two countries are exactly alike, I have enough experience to know how these places work, and to understand the *latino* temperament."

"Thank you," Santiago said, resentment dawning in his soul. "Thank you very much."

"I want you to consider me a friend, somebody in whom you can confide. When you're in doubt, don't hesitate to contact me, I beg you." Hamilton stood up. "I want to show you the house. Please, come with me."

He swung a door open and led Santiago into the residential wing. "I've always thought that Colombians live very well, don't you? The architect who designed this building was a real artist. There's no city in the world like Bogotá. Of all the cities I've lived in, Bogotá is my favorite."

The rooms were all painted in garish colors that were clearly the inspiration of a decorator. Santiago asked the ambassador about a canvas—entirely white—that hung on the wall.

Hamilton shook his head as if in exasperation. "That's a donation from a local artist who specializes in 'minimal art.' Between us, I'd say his brain is minimal, too. My wife's the artistic one—she has many painter friends. Me, I like to read for relaxation—science fiction especially. Maybe that's why I like your country so much." Hamilton's eyes widened with excitement. "Did you know that they've spotted more UFOs in Colombia than in California? I would give *anything* to visit that San Augustín park. From what I'm told, every afternoon there are reports of sightings. It's too bad Washington is against my trip there. I don't like to criticize my own government, but—Christ! Their caution seems a little excessive. If we want to maintain our supremacy, we have to conquer space. Our glory lies in technology. I'm completely convinced that Colombia is the key place from which to establish communications with extraterrestrials."

They entered the kitchen, and the ambassador, to Santiago's surprise, threw himself enthusiastically into a demonstration of how to use a food processor. Then he opened the door to an exterior garden. The rain had stopped, but everything was still wet and an icy breeze was blowing from the mountains. Trees shaded bushes from which hung many varieties of orchids. Hummingbirds danced wildly, pausing occasionally to drink, their wings invisibly fanning the air.

"Do you like orchids?" Santiago asked, feeling mischievous.

"Yes, they're gorgeous. Colombian orchids are the most beautiful in the world. Bogotá must have the perfect conditions for growing them. If you're interested, my wife is the real expert. She knows the name of every strain."

They strolled among peach trees, raindrops glistening on the blond hair of the fruit, then over wet grass to the edge of a cliff a few hundred feet above the city. The sun was a dull white disk just above the cloudy horizon.

"I'm glad we understand each other," Hamilton said. "Washington has to continue its public war against drugs. The cigarette companies and the banks are lobbying to legalize marijuana. After what's happened with oil and the Arab countries, nobody wants to depend on imports. The *sin semilla* they produce in my country— in Florida, California, and Pennsylvania—is better than anything you've got in Colombia. But don't think our motives are purely mercenary. We want to cooperate with you—with the Colombian government. I realize that this government's big worry is subversion. If you're willing to cooperate, it's in my power to have my friends in Washington send ammunition, maybe even advisers, to wipe out the terrorists. Don't forget—I have a lot of experience in this field, and my tenure in Chile and Paraguay was most successful. If I didn't have all this know-how, I wouldn't be here. Lean times are coming."

This sounded like a threat to Santiago, but he wasn't sure. "Yes, I'm afraid so," he echoed.

"That's right," the ambassador said solemnly. "I see you understand, my dear young *amigo*."

A security guard arrived on the run. The ambassador frowned, looked around, then nodded.

"Ambassador Hamilton," the guard puffed. "An urgent call for you from the State Department."

"Excuse me for a minute," said Hamilton.

Santiago looked at the plain below, sipped his drink, and thought of Beatrice. If he hadn't met her in Washington years ago, she probably would be alive now. As he stared into the savannah, the gray clouds opened and the sun burst through the monotonous afternoon; the city glowed in a golden mist. Is this what the conquistadores saw when they arrived four hundred years ago? Santiago wondered. A city whose trees bore golden fruit; a city that at sunset turned to gold? The El Dorado days were not over, he felt. Far from it. But the precious metal wasn't to be found at the bottom of the earth, as the Spaniards had thought. Maybe it fell, as the Indians had believed, from the sky, as invisible rain.

Thick dark clouds advanced upon the plain and covered the sun. Santiago felt chilly and alone: on the brink of a future he had never wanted and for which he wasn't prepared.

III
THE RETURN
OF THE
CADAVER

The city has been thrown into considerable excitement lately by a
difficulty between the *cachacos*
and the *ruanas*. The former means
the better dressed young men and the
latter, the class of people who wear
ruanas. . . .
There was an altercation yesterday
between the two groups; stones were
thrown, the military called. Some
two or three were killed and a number
wounded. But with a little management,
all this might have been avoided. As
it is, I presume it will be a day or
two before everything is settled.

FREDERIC EDWIN CHURCH
in a letter to his father
Bogotá, June 9, 1853

10 ▽

Santiago spent the month of April setting up the ministry. To house it, the government bought a rambling turn-of-the-century building that had once been a Jesuit high school; it was located in the Candelaria, the colonial part of the city. Construction workers were commandeered to remodel the main offices. Since Santiago had had no government experience, Caridad took care of making the most important appointments.

Every morning, Santiago met with his assistant, Francisco Gutiérrez, to go over the ministry's upcoming official obligations and answer the correspondence that began flooding the office. It was a far from ideal arrangement; the thirty-year-old Gutiérrez was a beer-bellied thug whose one obsession was ridding the country of Reds. When Santiago asked Caridad to have him removed, she insisted that it was impossible.

One rainy afternoon Santiago's secretary announced that General Juan Raúl Roca had arrived. Santiago asked that he be shown in, and the general—in his late fifties and balding, with a long aquiline nose and dull brown eyes—entered. Like some cartoon generalissimo, he wore a full-dress military uniform; an array of medals, shields, and insignias dangled from his chest. He was in a hurry, he said. He handed Santiago a sealed envelope, told him that it contained a copy of the armed forces' new Security Statute and that Santiago was to read it on television the next day, shook his hand, and left. Santiago caught his breath; it would be his first official appearance as government spokesman.

He broke the wax seal with his letter opener and read the single typewritten page.

> The Ministry of Public Information of the Republic of Colombia, in accordance with the powers vested in it by the Constitution, and taking into consideration that during the last few months seditious forces have dealt a series of blows to the sovereignty of the government and the stability of national life, declares that:
>
> From this date forward, and for a legal period of three hundred and sixty days, the Ministry of Public Information and, through it, the Armed Forces have the power and duty to arrest, without respect to habeas corpus, any citizen suspected of subversion.

Santiago was shaken. I cannot panic, he thought. He picked up the receiver and invited Caridad and Mario to dinner.

That night, after Santiago suggested that the statute would "cause trouble," Caridad leaped up from the table and started shouting. "You fool. Don't you know anything? General Roca is the army's strongman. He's the real leader of Colombia. The civilian government is a front, just a front, you dope, for the military. What Roca wants, Roca gets."

Mario joined in. "People who don't do what they're told can have fatal accidents."

The following day Santiago, heavily sedated, appeared on TV to read Roca's message.

The reaction to the measure was quick. The opposition press was outraged: It explained in its editorials that the government was claiming the right to detain any citizen without allowing him to consult a lawyer, and that the police were no longer required to give the press the names of those arrested. During the following week, riots broke out all over the country. Public service vehicles were burned, stores were looted, and American consulates were stoned.

The reaction spiraled upwards. The President shut down the universities and declared a nine-o'clock curfew in effect throughout the country. In Bogotá alone, the army made hundreds of arrests. A copy of a memo from General Roca was delivered to Santiago. It defined as "suspect of subversion" any artist, university professor, or student; any individual who did not belong to one of the traditional political parties; any antinationalists; and anyone who, in any way, protested the status quo.

One of the most unlikely people detained under the new law was an eighty-year-old surrealist poet, pulled by PAX agents from his bed, blindfolded, and interrogated. He had become suspect because each afternoon at sunset he stepped out onto his balcony and recited a text in a foreign tongue. The secret police, convinced this was a subversive harangue, did not believe him when he told them he was reciting André Breton's *The Surrealist Manifesto*.

The poet was released. Many equally innocent detainees were not; the new ministry's empty rooms were quickly converted into cells. Soon the international news agencies were publishing sensationalist accounts of the atrocities being committed in the name of law and order, and Amnesty International had scheduled a visit to Colombia.

During this period Santiago began to snort cocaine before leaving for work in the morning. He was feeling more and more shut off from what was in principle his own ministry. Gutiérrez, it was becoming clear, was the military's lackey, and it was he, not Santiago, who was the ministry's strongman. Santiago decided to try to flesh out his figurehead role. As a first step, he thought, I ought to give the ministry's jails a personal visit.

He pulled himself together and notified Gutiérrez of his plans to visit the jails. Four fully armed guards spent that afternoon leading him up and down dark, airless corridors. Although he'd had access to reports in foreign periodicals, Santiago was amazed by the conditions. Hundreds of people were locked up in dirty cubicles with neither mattresses to sleep on nor blankets to protect them from the frigid nights. The damp, windowless cells were infested with fleas, ticks, and roaches, and fat spiders hung from flaky, termite-ridden ceilings; the smell of human waste permeated the air. In one cell an unconscious man hung from the ceiling by his ankles, his head like an enormous beet dripping blood. Santiago, with a sudden rush of anger, had a guard cut him down; the prisoner came to and stared at Santiago with eerie eyes. When he questioned Gutiérrez, the assistant shrugged. "That's Gonzalo Santos. He's considered one of the most dangerous subversives. We can't take any chances with him." That night, Santiago had a long nightmare. In it, thousands of starving rats and throngs of angry lepers chased him through a bloody maze.

The next morning, going through the prisoners' files he found only the most superficial information: name, birthdate, address (if known), marital status, and the nature of the crime—which, in most instances, was simply "subversion." He skipped lunch and read on until the late afternoon. Toward the end of the day, he came across one file that was much thicker than the others. The photograph in it showed a man in his late thirties with long hair, an unkempt beard, and a contemptuous expression. The prisoner's name was Gonzalo Santos, and on the cover of the file, written in large red letters, were the words *Muy peligroso*. This was the same Santos, Santiago realized, whom he had ordered cut down the day before. According to the information inside, Santos had been educated in the United States and after graduating from Yale had been named cultural attaché at the Colombian embassy in Moscow. He was also a writer who had written a satire entitled *One Hundred Years of Ineptitude*. He ordered more coffee, canceled his appointments and read.

After dinner that night, Santiago phoned Mario; but a maid told him that Señor Simán was out of town and not expected back soon. He started to dial Caridad, then hung up and drank a glass of cognac. He dialed again. The maid announced pertly that Doctora Bello was at a dinner party.

Santiago slammed down the receiver. He had run out of cocaine a few days before, and with Mario gone didn't know where to get more. Besides, he'd stayed in Bogotá because of Mario and Caridad, and now his friends seemed to be evading him. Could he have been tricked into taking a job that nobody else wanted? Did they know what was going on? He looked out the window at the interminable drizzle and decided to get drunk.

He slept badly, sweating and aching as if from malaria. Gonzalo Santos's eyes staring at him from the bottom of a pitch-dark pit flashed again and again. This must be cocaine withdrawal, he thought. At four A.M., he got up and searched the apartment. After fumbling through bureaus and bookcases he found a small flask that had once contained the powder. He scraped the inside of the bottle, held it to his nostrils, and inhaled deeply. Within a few minutes, he was calm. He greeted the first light of dawn gratefully, took a long, hot shower, and sat down in the dining room to wait for his morning coffee. By the third cup, deliciously brewed by the sleepy, impassive Blanca, he was ready to face the office.

It was still early when he arrived at the ministry; only the night guards and cleaning women were there. He sat at his desk, opened the dossier on Gonzalo Santos, and read it again. When his secretary arrived, Santiago asked her to have Francisco Gutiérrez report to him. Gutiérrez strolled in minutes later. Santiago indicated the Santos file. "Tell me more," he said.

Gutiérrez frowned and lit a cigarette. "As far as I'm concerned, he's nothing but a fucking communist."

"Yes, no doubt. But in this jail—"

"The ministry is not a common jail," Gutiérrez shot back. "In my opinion that's not how the government sees it."

Santiago raised his eyebrows. "What kind of subversive is he?"

"What does it matter? A subversive is a subversive."

". . . is a subversive," said Santiago.

"I beg your pardon, *Señor Ministro*." Gutiérrez straightened up in his chair and stubbed out the cigarette. "Gonzalo Santos is one of the most dangerous men in the country, one of the major threats to the Colombian nation and the Simán administration."

Santiago pressed on: "What group does he belong to? Could you tell me that much?"

The aide hesitated for a moment. "Sure, I'll tell you about this guy," he said finally. "The Santos family were among the people who signed our declaration of independence, and Gonzalo had the best this society had to offer. He was a socialist when he returned from the Soviet Union, but it was not held against him in the beginning. After all, President Simán himself was once quite a radical young man. All our politicians here were communists in their youth. So when he comes back from the Soviet Union, he writes a few books about educating the masses and gets offered the post of Minister of Education." The expression on Gutiérrez's face darkened. "In his first public speech he says that private and religious education should be abolished because they're reactionary and bourgeois. Needless to say, he gets canned before he can do any damage. Then he starts to hang out with hippies and anarchists and fairies and junkies. And around that time he writes his 'brilliant masterpiece.'" Gutiérrez leaned toward Santiago. "His family is quite happy that he is where he is—he cannot embarrass them any longer. He committed two unforgivable sins: He was disrespectful of authority, and he betrayed his class." Gutiérrez's eyes were shining as if he had a high temperature.

As evenly as he could, Santiago said, "I'd like to interview the prisoner."

Gutiérrez stood up. "Is that an order, *Señor Ministro?*" he asked.

"Yes, it's an order. I'd like to see him this morning."

"Of course," Gutiérrez muttered.

Twenty minutes later, Santiago received a telephone call from General Roca. "I'm calling," the general barked, "because I have heard that you plan to talk to Gonzalo Santos."

Santiago was startled by how quickly the news had traveled.

"You would do well to know," thundered the voice, "that he is one man I personally want to see rot in prison. Furthermore, my dear *Señor Ministro,* it is not your job to question the administration's decisions."

Tripping over his own tongue, Santiago began to explain, "*Mi general,* the reason I want to see him is . . ."

The general broke in. "Your job is to represent our policies, not to make friends with the subversives. The ministry is not a charity organization. *Adios.*" An abrupt click put an end to the conversation.

Santiago hit his intercom button to tell his secretary to summon Gutiérrez. As her voice came on, three soft knocks sounded on his door. "Come in," he said.

Francisco Gutiérrez entered the room, announced that the prisoner was outside, then disappeared. A man of medium build, hunched over and prematurely aged, his head bandaged with bloody rags, trudged in and stood by the door.

There must be some mistake, Santiago thought. This looks like the wrong person. There was the full reddish beard, but this man looked much older than the one in the photograph. The prisoner stood frozen on the carpet, his head bent. Santiago stood up. Could this pitiful fellow be the feared Gonzalo Santos?

"Come in," Santiago said.

The prisoner stood as still as a statue.

"Please, come in and sit down." Santiago felt as though he were coaxing a reluctant pet.

The prisoner moved with great difficulty, as if he were in acute pain. His hands in his pockets, he shuffled across the room and dropped into a chair, then raised his head and stared at Santiago. Now Santiago knew he had the right man; there was no mistaking those penetrating eyes. But unlike the eyes that had lit his nightmares, Santos's actual eyes seemed empty of hatred.

"Would you like some coffee?" Santiago asked.

Gonzalo Santos nodded almost imperceptibly. Through the intercom, Santiago asked for two coffees. The prisoner fixed his eyes on him. They're like laser beams, thought Santiago. Santos's ravaged face was ghostly white, the lines in his forehead deep, as if he had been frowning for years. The secretary entered, set a tray on the desk, and left. Santiago took one cup and indicated that Santos should help himself to the other. The prisoner studied the cup on the tray but did not pick it up.

"Do you take milk and sugar?" Santiago asked.

"Black is fine, thank you." His voice was hoarse and raspy. With great effort, Santos pulled his hands from his pockets and reached for his cup. His hands were ulcerated stumps. Two chocolate-colored, dry-looking fingers like smoked bananas hung on to his right hand from threads of rotten flesh. Only the palms and thumbs of both hands were healthy. The rest of the skin was eaten away by what might have been a vicious leprosy. He held the cup between his palms. To fight off nausea, Santiago lit a cigarette.

"It isn't leprosy," Santos said, as if he had read Santiago's mind. "It's the paraffin."

Santiago had read newspaper and magazine articles about paraffin torture, but when he had confronted Caridad, she had sworn the stories were only propaganda spread by communists from Amnesty International. "Has the prison doctor seen you?" he asked.

Gonzalo Santos's lips curved into an ironic smile. "It's too late. The only thing a doctor could do now is amputate these two fingers." He rested the cup on the table and dangled his right hand in front of Santiago's eyes. "Besides, your Dr. Frankenstein is not here to cure anybody."

Gonzalo Santos smiled, revealing a row of caramel-colored teeth that was punctuated with black holes. He let the silence hang and looked out the window at the mountains; his eyes grew misty.

"Are you . . . are you . . . a terrorist?" Santiago asked, realizing the idiocy of his question even as he spoke.

Santos turned to look at him, his eyes glassy as if retaining the image of the mountains. He said nothing and looked away.

Santiago stood up and paced the office, forgetting Santos for a moment. He stopped in front of the window, turned around, and asked: "What is the paraffin torture? And who tortured you?"

Santos's eyes widened in disbelief. "*El Señor Ministro* doesn't know?"

Santiago answered angrily, "There is a lot I don't know." An ironic look crossed Santos's face. Then, clearing his throat, he said, "It's what they call the gauntlet test; it's a way of proving that someone has fired a gun. After a revolver discharges, traces of gunpowder are left on the hands. Paraffin detects it."

Santiago sat down again, rested his elbows on the desk, and leaned forward. "And every time they give this test the prisoner gets burned?"

Santos smiled almost indulgently. "No, no," he said. "Usually the test is done with cold paraffin, but our . . . friends at PAX use it hot, very hot. The paraffin gets into your pores and . . ." He held out his hand again. "As you can see, it works."

A chill shook Santiago. "I'll have a real doctor see you today."

"I'm not the only one with mutilated fingers," Santos said. "There are hundreds, maybe thousands."

"You mean being tortured?"

"Yes, tortured by PAX agents under orders from Caridad Bello."

Santiago stiffened. "Caridad Bello?"

"Yes, the one and only Caridad Bello. Her excellency Doctora Bello. She should remember what Octavio Paz said: 'Victims breed executioners.' "

Santiago was confused and shocked. "Is he also a subversive writer?" he asked moronically.

Gonzalo spat.

Santiago suddenly felt exhausted. He could think of nothing to say. He sat still, examining the ruined prisoner across from him. Then he hit the intercom for Gutiérrez and ordered him to have Santos transferred to a clean cell with a bed, latrine, and windows. "The interview is over," he said. "You may take the prisoner. Arrange for a private doctor to treat his wounds."

Alone in his office, Santiago stared at the wall and tried to regain control of himself. Could what Santos said about Caridad be true? Even as he asked the question, he knew the answer. At noon, he told his secretary to cancel his remaining appointments and had his driver take him home. The rain had grown heavy; a dense fog swathed the mountain peaks. He would have to get cocaine. He would ask Caridad.

Blanca, busy vacuuming, was disconcerted by his arrival; he usually let her know if he was coming home for lunch. Since the rape, their interaction had become increasingly tense. Santiago was beginning to fear that she might be a spy sent by PAX, and he considered replacing her with a daytime maid.

"Is Don Santiago going to have lunch here?" she asked.

"No, no, thank you." He felt like an intruder in his own home. "I'm not hungry." He poured himself a cognac.

"Would he like a cup of coffee, then?"

"Yes, that's fine," he said, wondering if the girl could be slowly poisoning him to get even. He would surreptitiously dump the coffee in a flowerpot.

From the kitchen, Blanca called out, "A messenger

brought a package for you this morning. It's on the dining-room table."

Santiago thanked her absentmindedly and turned on classical music to block out the frantic tropical rhythms blasting from the kitchen radio.

The cognac had a narcotic effect. Santiago's mind lingered on the image of Gonzalo Santos's putrid fingers. What Santiago found most alarming was Caridad's involvement. How had she gotten that job? How had she risen so fast? What kind of woman could perform torture routinely, with the same disinterest other people show in regular jobs?

His hands trembling, he reached for the telephone and dialed her number. When her line started ringing, he hung up. He downed the rest of his drink and dialed again.

"Hello," said Caridad.

He stalled. How would he begin? How *could* he? He began to regret having called.

"Who is this?" she said. He found the metallic tone of her voice both alluring and repellent.

"Caridad . . ."

"Santiago, darling, is that you?"

Santiago's heart was pounding. "Yes."

"What's up? Is anything wrong?" she asked.

"I don't know," he said, strangling on his own voice.

"Anyway, I was about to call you," she went on. "I just walked in from the office. I had a nasty, nasty morning. This weather . . . yuk."

Santiago decided to retreat. "I can call you later if you're busy now."

"Don't be silly. It's lovely to hear from you."

Despite her friendliness and warmth, her voice had

harsh undertones. She could still be at work, talking to one of her employees, thought Santiago. His mind went blank; he felt paralyzed.

"What are you doing tomorrow afternoon?" Caridad asked. Before he could answer, she continued, "Are you game for a ride in the country?"

The invitation caught him off guard. "I can be free. Sure, that sounds terrific," he managed to say.

"I'll pick you up at your office around three. Okay?"

"Okay."

"See you then, *corazón. Hasta mañana.*"

As Santiago hung up he noticed the parcel on the dining-room table, a small box wrapped in coarse yellow paper and sealed with adhesive tape. He opened it and found a watch case. Puzzled, he looked at the wrapper again. His name was clearly printed on it in a large bold hand. Lifting the boxtop he found a note that read:

Don't fuck with terrorists. Compliments of the cadaver.

The package fell from his hands. A strange object rolled out onto the spotless white tablecloth: a gnarled, shriveled finger wearing his father's emerald ring. Santiago gulped, gasped, then howled. The door opened behind him. "*¿Qué pasa*, Don Santiago?" Blanca called.

Santiago managed to grab the finger before she had a chance to see it.

"It's nothing," he struggled to say. "I'm sorry I frightened you. You may go."

When he heard the whir of the vacuum cleaner in the hall, Santiago hurried to his bedroom and locked the door. Close to vomiting, he flung the finger on the bed. Although motionless, it seemed to beckon to him. He took out his handkerchief, grabbed the chunk of flesh, and carried it to the bathroom, where he dropped it into the toilet. The finger floated for an instant, then sank. Santiago pushed down the lever. The bowl emptied and began to refill: the finger resurfaced. He clenched his teeth and pressed the lever again, this time holding it down. The finger vanished. Holding the handkerchief by one corner, Santiago set it on fire with his lighter and dropped it into the metal wastebasket next to the toilet. It fell like a parachute aflame. He watched it burn to nothing, then turned on the faucet, put his hands under the tap, and soaked, scrubbed, and rinsed them in scalding water.

11 ▽

After a restless night, Santiago arrived at his office at seven A.M. He stood by the window. For once, it was a clear morning; the green mountains were bathed in a warm, golden glow. Impatiently he waited until eight when the prison warden arrived and ordered an escort to take him to Gonzalo Santos's new cell. They climbed to the fourth floor; Santiago told the guard to unlock the door and wait.

The room was large, damp, and the ceiling beams were exposed. The walls had been given a coat of white paint that didn't quite cover the anti-Yankee, antigovernment graffiti beneath. No attempt had been made to clean the wooden floor. Morning light filtered through the bars over the one small window; the view included treetops and mountains. In one corner, a jug of water and a washbowl rested on a small table; beside it stood a bed. On it lay the prisoner.

Santos was sleeping soundly, but a sharp sound whistled with every breath from deep inside his lungs. Santiago placed the room's only chair next to Santos and sat down. With the sun's rays warming it, the cell seemed oddly peaceful.

From outside came the sounds of morning traffic: cars, buses, motorcycles, burros, and mule carts crisscrossing the narrow streets. Santiago got up and stood by the window. The sun had grown white; its sharply angled rays brought out the crevices and contours of the mountains. He turned around; Gonzalo Santos was awake. How long has he been watching me? Santiago wondered. "I came to see if they carried out my instructions," he said.

Santos raised himself up by the elbows and pulled his arms out from under the blankets; his hands were bandaged with clean gauze. "Your doctor amputated the rotten fingers . . . and I feel much better." He wiggled his thumbs, his pained expression momentarily gone.

Santiago sat down. "I'm glad you're feeling better. I'll make sure the doctor comes to see you every day." He scanned Santos's face, uncertain why this one prisoner's misery moved him so. Santos stared back without blinking.

"I told you yesterday—this jail is full of half-dead people. Sometimes the fleas, the cold, and hunger keep me awake. But what drives me crazy is the piercing screams; they're like needles piercing my brain."

"How long have you been here?" Santiago asked.

Santos squinted vacant-eyed into space. A moment passed. "Do you have a cigarette?" he asked.

Santiago lit a cigarette and placed it between Santos's

lips. The man pushed it to a corner of his mouth with his tongue and inhaled. The cigarette tilted down, almost singeing his ragged beard.

"I'd say it's been a few months," he began, "but I've lost count. At first I used to hear from my friends on the outside, and I kept up with the news from newspapers I came across. I don't know. . . . For a while I kept track of the days, but when I was moved from cell to cell, it was hard to be sure. Then they started with the paraffin. . . . Months. At least a few months." He paused, his eyes losing themselves in memory. "I would assume this is May."

"The end of May," Santiago said.

Santos's eyes wandered over the walls of his new cell. Santiago took the cigarette, flicked the ash into the empty washbowl, and placed it back between Santos's lips.

"Thank you," he said. His voice was quivering. "Thank you very much. Now let me see . . ." He drew the last word out into a low hum.

Santiago interrupted him. "There is one more thing I have to know. Are you a member of F-69?"

"Who? Me?" he snorted. As he burst out laughing, he choked on smoke and coughed. The cigarette fell from his mouth, rolled down his beard, and landed on his bare chest. Santiago snatched it away. Santos stopped coughing; his eyes were bloodshot. "I don't want to burn anymore," he muttered. "No, I've never been a member of any group like that."

"Then why were you arrested?"

"In a country like this who knows? In the beginning it wasn't bad, there were strange types around. You know their families come to visit them on Sundays and bring them newspapers and lunches. A boiled potato, some rice, a marrow bone. Delicious. But it can all change in a minute. One day they are pals, the next day they kill each other over a cigarette or a joint." He pointed to the window, "In Colombia you're a prisoner whether or not you're in jail."

Back in the office, Santiago told his secretary he did not want to be disturbed by any calls or visitors. He sat at his desk or paced around the room and chain-smoked. At lunch hour, when his subordinates left for nearby restaurants, he stayed inside, his mind racing.

He waited anxiously for Caridad to arrive. At three o'clock, he left his office and went through the building's main entrance and out into the street. The day was sunny, the cobalt blue sky cloudless. It was warmer now; Santiago stripped off his jacket, loosened his tie, and lit a cigarette. He felt nervous. People entering and leaving the building seemed to be looking at him strangely. In recent weeks, paranoia had begun gripping him at unexpected moments. He wondered if it was his appearance that was making everyone stare. He knew he had lost weight; the staples of his diet were coffee, cognac, vodka, and cigarettes. His face was drawn; his eyes felt oddly dry, as if his pupils were dilated. His paranoia accelerated. Could everyone have somehow heard about what he had done to Blanca? Could they have found out about his father's murder? Santiago shook his head, as if to shake off his fears.

A car's horn sounded. He threw down his cigarette

and walked toward Caridad's gleaming red Alfa Romeo. Before he settled back into the seat, Caridad pressed down the accelerator; Santiago's head hit the headrest.

"What were you thinking about?" she asked. "You looked as if you were a million miles away."

He looked her over intently. Today she wore a red silk blouse, a black chamois jacket, white cotton slacks, snakeskin riding boots, and no makeup; false eyelashes set off her jade eyes. He looked away. Despite her extraordinary beauty, there was an austere masculine quality about her.

She turned onto a steep, narrow cobblestone street and headed toward the mountains.

"You have to make the most of this weather," she said. "There are so few good days that whenever I can I sneak away for a drive in the country. It's the only way I can escape the madness at the office." Santiago noticed that she said "the office" the way any lady executive would refer to the place where she worked.

Traffic on the highway was light. The road, cut into the mountain ridges, climbed steadily. Through the row of eucalyptus trees flashed glimpses of the city, hundreds of feet below.

Half an hour later the Alfa was deep in the country, whipping through hamlets and villages whose streets were empty save for burros and mules; through corn, potato, *arracacha,* and wheat fields crowded with toiling peasants; past dairy farms, granaries, ponds, and dense forests.

They drove for most of the afternoon. The speed and the countryside relaxed Santiago, but Caridad remained silent. Finally, she pulled over and stopped at a roadside inn.

There were no other customers. From a table on a rustic wooden terrace abloom with geraniums, begonias, and orchids, they could see a pasture and the blue mountains behind it. Caridad ordered strawberries and cream for the two of them. Santiago decided to let her begin the conversation.

"So what's going on, sweetheart?" Caridad asked mock-sweetly. "I mean, other than making friends with prisoners."

Santiago watched Caridad's long black fingernails as she brought a berry to her mouth and bit into it.

He was about to reply but remained silent.

She dangled the half-eaten berry before her and gazed at it dreamily. "I suggest that you don't cross Juan Raúl," she said. "He's not the forgiving type, and besides, I understand you've already insulted him. You really are a slow learner, aren't you? Listen to me. Juan Raúl is the army's strongman. That means he makes the rules." She extended her tongue and placed the fruit on it.

"What about the President?"

"Mario's father isn't much more than a puppet—everybody knows that. The army likes to have a President. It's good public relations. That way we can all pretend we have a democracy." She shrugged. "If you don't believe me, ask Mario—he should know."

"But I thought—"

"Look, Santiago," she interrupted. "Leave the thinking to the two-bit intellectuals this hick country is so full of. You and I are better off tending to our interests. And we don't have much besides the army to protect us from the terrorists." She snorted at his surprise. "And don't get all romantic about terrorists. What do you think it is that they want—justice and equality for all? You make me laugh, you're such a child. It's power—*our* power—that they're after. So when the army makes a suggestion, let's play ball. Juan Raúl told me—"

"You know the general?"

Caridad looked fierce. "Of course I know him. I've known him since I was fourteen years old. I had no choice; he was my father's best friend. How, my darling, do you think I got so far so fast?"

Santiago took a deep breath. "But torture . . ." he began.

Caridad whooped. "Oh, poor baby. I'd forgotten your long-standing hatred of brutality and your passionate commitment to human rights." She touched his arm. "In your so-called civilized countries, they have other kinds of torture. 'Brutality' is just a word the *gringos* use to justify their image of us as savages."

Santiago pulled his arm away. "Gonzalo Santos told me . . ."

Caridad interrupted. "Forget that asshole or you're going to end up in jail yourself." She reached out and took his chin. "Look, my pet, Colombians don't think torture is such a big deal. Don't forget: It began with the Indians. They committed suicide because they knew they would pass into a better life. People here know they will be rewarded for their suffering—in the next life, not this one." She pushed aside her bowl. "Waiter," she called. "Check."

Santiago reached for his wallet.

"Never mind," she said, digging into her bag and flinging pesos on the table, "I've got it."

As they made their way toward the car, the sun hung low in the sky, and a full moon, white as a bleached skull, was rising behind the lapis-lazuli mountains.

As Caridad drove back onto the highway, she turned to Santiago and asked, "Have you ever been to the crater at El Dorado?"

Santiago, dazed, shook his head.

"Why don't we go over there?" Caridad said. Her voice was suddenly cheerful. "It's a terrific place. One of my favorites."

She braked, spun the car around, and took off in the opposite direction. Within half an hour they were on a steep, bare, rocky mountain road bereft of vegetation except for white velvet *frailejones,* moss, and purple *mora* berries. Caridad slowed down and pulled over.

"This is as far as we can go by car. We have to walk the rest of the way. Come on." She jumped out.

She walked briskly and surefootedly. Like a mountain goat, Santiago thought. Then his ears popped, and he arrived abruptly at the edge of a crater. It looked like a hollow dug by a meteor; its sides were alive with lichen and flowers of the *paramo*. The lake within reflected the pale yellow of the sky. Caridad ambled along the water's edge and squatted on a rock. Santiago sat on the moss next to her, struggling to recover his breath.

"Isn't this beautiful?" she asked, arching her back. "This is where the Zipa chief, covered with gold dust, came once a year to plunge into the water. It's where the Indians made their sacrifices to the sun and moon. I like to come here whenever I can. It's as if the place were still breathing." Her gaze drifted across the water's surface.

Santiago found the place ghostly. He looked around, noticing a large bush some three yards tall with bell-shaped Prussian-blue flowers the size of avocados. The pistils of the flowers were a deep topaz.

"What gorgeous flowers," he said.

Caridad glanced at him. "They are called *borracheros* —drunkards." She got up and plucked two of them. "They smell nice too." She sniffed one, then the other, then held them out to Santiago. "Smell. The Indians ate these during their ceremonies." She ripped off a petal. "Want a taste?" She placed one in her mouth.

Santiago took the other flower and imitated her. They chewed in silence. The petals released a bittersweet, creamy juice like the *curuba* fruit. Before they had finished, Santiago began to feel dizzy. Caridad stretched herself out on her back and watched the clouds whirling through the sky.

"What a high," she said softly. "It's better than grass or coke or vodka. What a divine high. *Absolutamente divina*." She laughed.

Santiago laughed, too. He felt as if he were rising above the mountains, no longer touching earth. He shut his eyes and saw a transparent sea, filled with snails and coral and fish; at its bottom, skeletons were guardians of a gold treasure. He felt his body lose all gravity and his spirit leave him to explore the shores of the lake and the mountains. He opened his eyes and moved closer to Caridad. If my spirit is elsewhere, he thought, then I can say anything I want to this woman without fear of harm.

"I've been thinking about leaving Colombia again," he said. He seemed to hear his own voice echoing along the mountain range. "This job is too much for me. I'm not used to . . . torture. I don't like it. Besides, since my father's death, I haven't been able to get sexually aroused. Except with the maid . . . the maid, Blanca, and I . . . we . . . you know. I spent the whole night snorting coke. . . ." He thought he had lost all his inhibitions, but something stopped him from a complete confession.

Caridad sat up and placed her index finger on his lips. "I know all about it, *corazón*. And I know what your problem is. In Bogotá, passion is a measure of the intensity of one's loneliness." She smiled. "PAX has little machines that keep us informed. Just think what would have happened if the Indians had had tape recorders and electronic spy systems. Things would have been so different. Nothing gets by me, my dear Santiago. Don't forget, I'm like a mother to you. When you want something, tell me. At PAX we've got people who have to be destroyed anyway."

Santiago realized that he had expected her to know about Blanca. He stared at the lake. In the center of it he imagined a fountain of fresh, scarlet blood, and lost himself in the vision.

"I've always believed that the Indians had some very good ideas," Caridad went on. "Human sacrifice, for example. It is an ancient necessity. It's something you and I have in our blood; we can't deny it." She leaned over Santiago. Her eyes reflected the opalescent gold of the lake. "I practice human sacrifice," she said. Santiago felt neither shock nor horror—just awe. "Opening a human chest, *incroyable*. Thrusting your hands inside and tearing out a beating heart." Her fervor made her look like a crusader. "It makes you realize that we're all the same. Everybody. Every one of us." Her eyes closed in ecstasy, she smiled slightly and stood up.

Santiago continued to look at her. She seemed to have grown several feet taller; her short hair seemed to have grown to her waist. When he reached out like a child to touch it, Caridad's cold hand pulled him to his feet.

"Where are we going?" he said.

"I have someone tied up in the trunk," she said. "It's a prisoner Juan Raúl wants us to get rid of. Come. Give me a hand."

Santiago looked up at the reddening sky and thought he understood now the meaning of this landscape. Caridad was walking purposefully toward the car. He followed her.

12 ▽

Santiago didn't return to the office for the rest of the week. He stayed at home listening to music, drinking cognac, and snorting cocaine from the new cache Mario had dropped off. In the evenings, he stood on the terrace, wrapped in a heavy *ruana* to protect himself from the chilly Bogotá night, and wondered if the incident at the lake had really taken place or if it had been a drug-inspired hallucination. Whenever he tried to sleep, he saw Caridad's hands dig into the prisoner's open chest and tear out a palpitating heart.

At two A.M. the next Friday, he was lying groggy but awake in bed when the telephone rang. Alarmed, he picked up the receiver.

"Did I wake you?" asked Caridad.

"No, no. What's the matter?" This wouldn't be a social call.

"It's F-69. They dug a tunnel to the military barracks and tied up the guards who must have been drunk as hell. They stole millions of dollars' worth of weapons. Imagine all that ammunition in the hands of fanatics!"

"Oh my God."

"We can't waste time being amazed. Meet me in your office in half an hour. *Ciao*."

When he arrived twenty minutes later, Santiago found Caridad already there, talking on the telephone and filing her fingernails with a vengeance. She had her feet propped up on the cluttered desk and looked as impeccable as if she had just come from the hairdresser. Seconds after Santiago came in, she hung up and stashed the nail file in her bag.

She gestured to the table and said, "There's a thermos of coffee over there. Have some, you'll need to be wide awake. We have to decide right now whether we're going to notify the press or keep this a secret."

Santiago poured himself a cup while Caridad stared at him, her eyes like radiant agates.

"That was Juan Raúl on the phone. He's really pissed off. The army's afraid this thing will make them the laughingstock of Colombia."

Santiago choked down some coffee and lit a cigarette.

"What happens now?" he asked.

"We take action, that's what happens. We're supposed to be after the terrorists, not vice versa. I just don't know what action to take. They've got our weapons."

"What did General Roca say?"

"Fuck him. He wants to wash his hands of the whole thing and keep it quiet." She stood up and poured herself another cup of coffee.

"And the President?" Santiago asked.

Caridad wheeled around sharply. "The President can't do anything," she cried. The cup rattled against the saucer, spilling coffee on her blouse. *"Mierda,"* she said, close to tears. "My new Halston blouse." She stared at Santiago. "How many times do I have to tell you—it's the generals who run this country."

Santiago shifted in his seat. "Why don't we call Mario? He's the one who got me into this mess in the first place."

Caridad looked at him incredulously. "I've already called Mario," she said. "He'll be here as soon as he can screw his leg on. He may have an idea—he usually does. So far we haven't done too well." She flung the coffee cup across the room; it broke against the wall. "Goddam this country."

The door opened and Mario appeared, limping more than usual. His eyes were bulging and his face looked puffy; Santiago decided he must have hurried from a cocaine orgy.

"I should be the Minister of Public Information *and* the chief of PAX. Or at least get your salaries," Mario said. "This country would fuckin' fall apart without me."

"Okay, wise guy, what have you come up with?" Caridad's eyes flashed. "Are you all right, or are you high?"

"Both."

"Just terrific!" she snarled. "Now we're really screwed."

"But you like getting screwed." He waved his arms like an orchestra conductor. "I have a brilliant idea. We'll show those motherfuckers."

"Sure," she grumbled. "How?"

Mario waved one arm at Santiago. "Unless some of us have ethical objections."

"Fuck ethical objections," Caridad broke in. "War is war."

Mario leaned against the desk and said, "Okay. Who else knows about this?"

Caridad thought for a few seconds. "The soldiers at the barracks. My assistants. Juan Raúl. That's all."

Mario stared at Santiago and said, "We need a dozen prisoners. Have them dressed as soldiers and send them to the garrison in a patrol car. They must be there in half an hour." He pointed to the telephone. Santiago paused. "Dial, dammit," Mario ordered.

Santiago lifted the receiver and gave Mario's order to the head guard of the night shift. Mario turned to Caridad. "Call General Roca and tell him we need his help. Tell him to call the barracks and give orders that when we make the scene, the officers will do what they're told, no questions asked."

She picked up the phone to dial the general's number, but stopped short. "What's the plan, Mario?" she said. It was the first time Santiago had ever heard apprehension in her voice.

"You'll see. Come on, get moving."

The general's line was busy for ten agonizing minutes; when she finally got through, the conversation was brief.

"We're in," she said as she hung up. "He'll do it. Now what?"

"That's it," said Mario, puffing up like a turkey. "Let's split."

They decided to ride in Caridad's car. It was a clear, dry night, and the streets were empty. Within twenty minutes they had arrived at the barracks entrance. The guard waved and let them pass. Caridad braked to a halt in front of the brightly lit main building as an officer came out to meet them.

"Captain Quiñones, at your service." He saluted. "General Roca called to say you were on your way."

Once inside the building, Mario spoke with an authority Santiago had never witnessed in him before.

"I want all military personnel off the premises right now," he ordered. "But keep it quiet. I'll need one submachine gun, a dozen grenades, and a half-dozen dynamite sticks."

Quiñones saluted and marched out of the office. A patrol car pulled up to the building. A teenager in uniform pushed open the door and addressed Santiago. "The prisoners you asked for are here, *Señor Ministro*," he said.

Mario stood in front of the boy. "Are they secure?"

"Yes, sir. The door is locked." He waved the key in the air; Mario took it.

"Go join the others."

"Yes, doctor," the boy said.

Within twenty minutes, all military personnel had been evacuated from the garrison. Mario carried the submachine gun Quiñones had brought him and handed Colt .45s to Caridad and Santiago. Outside, a chilly predawn breeze was blowing down from the mountains. Mario ordered Santiago to unlock the door of the van while he and Caridad stood directly across from it, some fifty yards away. Santiago obeyed mechanically, then joined his friends.

"Listen to me, men," Mario shouted. "Get out of that truck one at a time. Any tricks and you're dead."

A young man, his eyes wide with terror, showed his close-cropped head. Someone behind gave him a push and he popped out of the truck like an ostrich chick from its egg and fell to the ground. He pulled himself up and staggered toward Mario.

"Okay. Keep moving. Next," Mario bellowed.

The rest of the prisoners, in makeshift military uniforms, emerged from the van. They murmured nervously among themselves, nudging each other like caged animals.

"Listen carefully," Mario said. The whispering ceased. "I'm going to count to three. When I start counting, run for your lives. Anyone who gets away is free." He pointed the machine gun at the group. "One . . . two . . ."

Santiago spotted Gonzalo Santos among the prisoners and pushed the barrel of Mario's gun toward the ground. Mario slammed the butt of the gun against Santiago's forehead and began firing. Santiago felt blood pour from his head. His vision grew fuzzy, and he fell to the ground.

"They're getting away," Caridad shouted, firing wildly.

Mario hobbled after the fleeing prisoners. His machine gun barked out a fan of flames; the prisoners yelped in pain as they fell wounded and dead. Santiago tried to get up, but his eyes were still clouded with blood. Caridad stomped on his chest, forcing him back to the ground. "If you move, faggot, I'll blow your brains out," she snarled.

A minute later, the tempest of bullets had ceased. Mario, limping and panting, threw his machine gun aside.

"Get up, you dumb fuck," he snapped. "Do you realize what you've done? One of the prisoners escaped."

Santiago rose slowly. "Don't worry, Mario," he said.

"I'll accept the responsibility for everything that went wrong."

"You sure as hell will," Mario said. "I'm not going to pay for your stupidity. *You* explain this to the generals." He reached into a wooden crate and began handing Santiago and Caridad grenades and sticks of dynamite. "Let's get this over with. Scatter the bodies, set them on fire, and meet me at the entrance in five minutes." He turned to Santiago. "No more screwups from you, asshole."

Loaded with ammunition, they went off in separate directions, dousing the corpses with gasoline and lighting matches to them. They planted explosives by two small dormitories and set them off; explosions shook the silence of the moonless, starry night. One by one, lights flickered on in the homes around the installation.

When the three met at the main entrance, the strong acrid smell of roast flesh saturated the air. Mario turned to Santiago and said, "Make up a list of eleven names for the media. We'll say that the prisoners were soldiers." Santiago felt nauseated. "Nobody is going to be able to recognize those charred bodies," Mario said scratching his head. "Let the newspapers and TV people come. We're blaming the massacre on F-69."

Caridad spat. "What a stench!" She held her nose.

A jeep stopped in front of the main entrance and Quiñones jumped out.

"Don Santiago will give you a list of the soldiers killed in the attack," Mario said to him. "We'll break the news to the media. Do you understand?"

"Yes, doctor, I understand," mumbled the captain, looking uncertainly at the bombed-out barracks.

Mario continued, "You can let the soldiers in now.

Have them put out the fire and pile the bodies together. These men were murdered by terrorist sons of bitches. They're heroes. Bury them with the highest honors."

At four in the morning, they returned to the ministry building. The sky was still wrapped in a black shroud. Mario and Caridad agreed that the most important next step was to prepare a press release for Santiago to read on television later that day. They worked tirelessly while Santiago looked on. By the time the sun rose from behind the mountains, painting them with faint subdued pastels, they had finished a satisfactory account of the assault on the garrison.

It was Caridad who drove Santiago to his penthouse. She waited while he showered and snorted more cocaine, helped him choose a suit, and escorted him to the studio. Makeup covered his cuts and bruises and the bags under his eyes. After several false starts, he managed to read the official version of what had happened the night before. Once the taping was over, Caridad took him home. In the lobby she said, "Listen, stupid. You'd better start dealing with reality. You're kidding yourself about a lot of things."

Back in the apartment, he looked for Blanca. The girl was gone, but her belongings were still in the bedroom. He spent the rest of the morning sprawled on his bed, dwelling with morbid pleasure on the punishment he would receive for letting the prisoner escape. Finally he yawned, unplugged the phone, set the alarm clock for six-thirty, took four barbiturates, and slept.

▼   ▼   ▼

It was dark when the alarm went off. Still sleepy, he washed his face and made himself a strong cup of coffee. Blanca had not reappeared. At seven, he turned on the TV and lay back on the sofa. The President's press secretary materialized, apologized for the interruption of regular programming, and announced that Dr. Santiago Villalba, Minister of Public Information, would address the Colombian nation to explain in full detail what had taken place at military headquarters earlier in the day.

Santiago watched himself appear behind a desk in front of the Colombian flag. He was wearing the black suit, light-blue shirt, and lilac tie that Caridad had chosen.

"Fellow Colombians," he heard himself say. "Since dawn, when the attack on military headquarters took place, the President's press secretary has kept you informed of the seriousness of the acts perpetrated during the past twenty-four hours."

Santiago nodded at himself. His TV incarnation, looking up during the pauses to emphasize the crucial points, was far more certain and emphatic than the real man ever felt.

"The bulletins obviously couldn't supply all the details of the incident. Now it is both possible and necessary to inform this nation and the concerned international community of the measures taken by the Colombian government regarding the subversive acts committed by F-69.

"The government understands that the violent attack on the barracks is part of the new war tactics that are being used by terrorist groups against democratically elected governments. War, however, does not always mean armed confrontations. It often manifests itself in the dangerous acts practiced by international terrorists. Unfortunately, it was Colombia's turn to be the site of a serious attack on the established forces of order.

"In addition to forcing their way into the barracks and

brutally slaughtering eleven soldiers on duty, setting their bodies on fire as they lay dying, this heinous group of criminals and delinquents who call themselves F-69 stole weapons valued at ten million dollars. These arms had been purchased by the government to put down sedition. F-69 has promised to strike again if we do not immediately release hundreds of common criminals whom they shamelessly refer to as 'political prisoners.' Among those whose freedom they call for are men and women convicted of kidnapping and murdering several prominent figures of Colombian society. Their list also includes many other prisoners already convicted and sentenced for bombings, extortion, and blackmail.

"We think it is important that you realize that these people are asking for the release not of a group of failed or harmless idealists, but of common criminals and assassins who know no moral bounds and whose crimes have been characterized by cruelty and brutality. The government, of course, will make every effort to find a solution that requires no bloodshed. . . ."

Santiago watched himself read, amazed that his body was the instrument that delivered those words, sentences, paragraphs. When the speech ended, the television image switched to the funeral services of the dead "soldiers" being lowered into eleven parallel graves. The announcer's voice explained that a monument would be erected on the site in memory of these men martyred defending the motherland. The Colombian flag was raised while the military band played the national anthem. In the background, cries of mourning could be heard. Santiago turned off the set and poured himself a double cognac.

▼ ▼ ▼

That night he couldn't sleep. He spent the long hours snorting cocaine, drinking, listening to melancholy Andean music, and thinking of Caridad. In spite of the hideousness of her nature and the abuse she directed at him, he felt obsessively drawn to her.

At seven A.M., Santiago was still alert. He was also uncontrollably jumpy—the cocaine was thick in his bloodstream. The apartment door opened. His panicky first thought was that a death squad was breaking in to assassinate him. Then Blanca walked into the room, whistling and carrying an armful of newspapers. She stopped dead in her tracks when she saw Santiago.

"*Buenos días,* Don Santiago. *¿Cómo . . . está?*" she asked, beaming.

"Where have you been all this time?" he asked harshly.

The girl blushed. "Doesn't Don Santiago remember that Saturday is my day off? I went to see my parents."

"Ah, sorry. I forgot."

"I brought your newspapers," she added. "Would you like a nice hot cup of coffee, sir?"

He stared at her without answering and held out his hand to take the papers.

Blanca disappeared into the kitchen, turned the radio on loud, and tuned to the news. The announcer rattled on while Santiago—his head as heavy as a bucket full of rocks—leafed through the newspapers. The account was described in words almost identical to those Santiago had used the night before. He examined the photos of the soldiers' burial and the devastated barracks and of himself making the television announcement. He dumped the papers on the rug and a mimeographed sheet slipped out of the pile. At the bottom of the page was a name he immediately recognized: Gonzalo Santos. He was still staring at the name when Blanca came in and announced, "Don Santiago, your coffee is ready."

"What? What?" he said. His hands were shaking and his eyes wouldn't focus.

"Your coffee, Don Santiago," the girl repeated, eyeing him.

"Oh, all right. Just leave it there." He lowered his voice. "And please, Blanca, turn down that radio."

The girl retreated silently. Santiago poured himself a cup of coffee but didn't drink it: Blanca's cheerfulness meant, he decided, that she was definitely trying to poison him. He turned back to Santos's memo. It described in detail the actual events of the massacre, and appealed to the Colombian people to participate at two that afternoon in a demonstration to protest the brutality of the government.

Santiago felt both proud and frightened by the memo —proof of Santos's survival. In his exhilaration he drank cup after cup of coffee. So what if Blanca is trying to poison me? he thought. At least death will end this nightmare. What could he do now? Obviously he couldn't call Mario. Maybe Caridad would talk.

"What's the matter, Santiago?" Caridad asked when he had dialed her number.

"I hope I didn't wake you."

"Me? Are you crazy? I get up at the crack of dawn."

"Caridad, did you hear about Gonzalo Santos?"

"Of course," she said shortly. After a few seconds' pause she spoke again. "It looks like the demonstration is going to be enormous. At the end of it the crowds are going to regroup around the bullfight ring, right by your building. If you want my advice, stay out of the streets today. It's going to get very, very ugly. I have to go now. *Ciao.*"

Santiago went into the bathroom, dug a powerful telescope out of the closet, set it up on the terrace, and took a look. The clarity and range were excellent. He could see all the way to La plaza del Capitolio, where the demonstration would begin.

Blanca served lunch at noon, but Santiago wasn't hungry. He sat on the terrace, swilling cognac. Clouds on the horizon threatened rain. He squinted through the telescope at the groups of people arriving at the square in buses and trucks. The crowd was already large. Hundreds of banners danced above it, too far away to read. According to the flier, the marchers would proceed up the Carrera Séptima. The street was lined with mounted policemen and with soldiers carrying clubs, machine guns, and rifles.

At exactly two o'clock, in this country where nothing ever worked on time, the march began. As it moved north, streams of people from the adjacent neighborhoods joined it. Not even the carnival in Barranquilla, when the entire city gathered in the streets for the Batalla de Flores, attracted so many people.

The demonstration advanced slowly. The marchers sang and shouted slogans; from this terrace Santiago couldn't make out the words. As he sat at the telescope, Blanca walked out next to him and stood a few yards away, looking through a pair of binoculars. Santiago wondered whether the girl wouldn't prefer to be part of the swelling crowd below.

"What are they shouting?" he asked.

"Bread. Water. Electricity," Blanca said without lowering the binoculars. "They're shouting because they don't have any, Don Santiago."

"They have no water?" he asked.

"No water, no electricity, no work, no food, nothing." She turned toward him. "Where my parents live they have to walk a mile to buy a gallon of water. And when you get there sometimes there isn't any."

Santiago shook his head, unsure whether or not to believe her.

"It's true," Blanca said tartly. She shrugged and looked back toward the crowd. It was about twenty blocks away.

Santiago could now read some of the black-and-white signs bobbing above the mass of heads: "Democracy yes. Militarization no." "Down with military brutality." "Revolutionary violence is the answer to reactionary violence."

The chanting and songs were growing louder. The first words Santiago made out were:

> The masses, united, will never be enslaved.
> The masses, united, will never be exploited.
> The masses, united, will never be conquered.

Santiago could now distinguish some of the demonstrators' faces. No one group seemed to predominate; all ages and social classes were represented. With a roar they raised their fists above their heads, and chanted slogans. Despite the gesture and the fervor of their words they seemed calm, almost happy. If these people got together to overthrow the government, nothing could stop them, he thought. If they have neither water nor electricity . . . their lives must be subhuman. They really have nothing to lose.

Part of the crowd took up the cry: "Simán, orangutan. Simán, Simán, chief of the clan. Simán, Simán, son of Uncle Sam."

Blanca lowered her binoculars and laughed; there was a happy defiance in her eyes.

"Brothers dead in the struggle, you'll live forever," another group shouted. As the crowd drew closer, more chants grew audible: "Oppressed workers, stick together." "Down with Yankee imperialism." *"Muera la burgesia."*

When the marchers began to climb the steep road that led to the bullring the cacophony resolved into a single cry, as if a signal had been passed among them. "Water, electricity! Water, electricity! Water! Water! Water!"

"Now come the speeches," Blanca said eagerly.

As the area in front of the bullring filled, Santiago amused himself by reading banners and placards: "The soil belongs to those who farm it." "United we shall overcome." "No more torture." "No more taxes." "Workers and students, unite!" "A united left will never be beaten." By the time the entire crowd had assembled, large clumps of marchers were holding hands and singing:

> "Arise, ye prisoners of starvation,
> Arise, ye wretched of the earth!
> For Justice thunders condemnation,
> A better world's in birth!"

One voice rose above the others. Santiago raised his eyes from the telescope; Blanca, her face flushed, was singing along. Santiago got up and went into the living room to freshen his drink. When he returned to the terrace, microphone stands and loudspeakers had sprouted below, and the other balconies and terraces of his building had filled with spectators; many, like Santiago, were drinking cocktails.

Looking through the telescope once more, a movement caught his eye. Inside the bullring, concealed from the crowd by baroque stonework, armed soldiers were setting up machine-gun positions. The barrels were aiming at the protestors.

"Oh my God," Santiago murmured. He took Blanca's arm and drew her to the telescope. "Look, the plaza is full of soldiers," he said.

Blanca's mouth opened in a slow, silent scream. She dropped the binoculars and ran from the terrace; before he could stop her, the door to the apartment slammed shut.

Santiago leaned down to look through the telescope. On an improvised wooden platform, a bearded young man was stepping to the microphones.

"Give me an R!" he shouted. His voice somehow soared above the shriek of feedback.

"R!" roared the crowd.

"Give me an E!"

"EEEEE . . ."

"Give me a V!"

"VEEEEE . . ."

"Give me an O!"

"OOOOOO . . ."

Santiago wheeled the telescope around and scanned the street. A skinny, lone figure was running downhill, her arms waving. "Blanca," said Santiago.

"¡*Revolución!*" the crowd shouted. "¡*Revolución!*" They turned to face Santiago's apartment complex, raised their fists, pointed their placards, and chanted: "There they are, the ones who sold the motherland. There they are. They're the ones." Santiago wondered why he felt no urge to duck and hide.

Through the telescope he tried to find Blanca again and couldn't. The man on the platform raised his arm, and when the crowd quieted, Gonzalo Santos took the microphone between his maimed hands. The crowd gave him a crazed ovation.

"Comrades," he said. His booming, amplified voice trembled. "The moment has arrived to—"

The soldiers opened fire. The people who were hit dropped to the ground like marionettes collapsing on stage. Those who escaped the bullets fled blindly in all directions like agitated ants. Santiago scanned the bullring; Santos had vanished.

The shooting didn't stop. People wheeled, struggled, crawled over each other, and dropped. The fury of the slaughter stunned Santiago beyond horror. Like a zombie he sat up, walked to his room, and sat on the edge of his bed. The pathetic screams and the persistent popping of the guns reached through the length of the apartment. He lay face down and, covering his ears with his palms, he buried his head under two pillows.

When he got up, half an hour later, the firing had stopped. He went back to the terrace; piteous cries and moans rose from the streets below. The sun was still shining, but a hard drizzle had begun to fall. Soldiers squatted on the steps of the plaza while hundreds of people searched the streets for relatives and friends.

Santiago went inside, poured himself a cognac, sat on the living-room sofa, and stared at the walls.

Some time later the telephone rang.

"May I speak with Dr. Villalba, please."

"Speaking."

"Dr. Villalba," said a man with a heavy accent, "this is Carl Crystal from the American embassy."

"Yes," Santiago said. "What can I do for you?"

"Ambassador Hamilton has called a meeting at his residence at eight-thirty tonight. It's absolutely essential that you come."

"Oh, a meeting, eh?"

Santiago dropped the phone and walked out of the room.

He found a bottle of white powder in the library, behind the collected works of Dickens. The image of mangled bodies and the sound of moaning spun in his head. He snorted cocaine until his nose bled.

13 ▽

By eight o'clock he was so high that the call from the doorman rattled him. Outside the building an official car, flanked by four cops on motorcycles, was waiting. The drizzle had stopped but the air was still damp, and a sharp, icy wind was blowing through the street deserted except for packs of hungry dogs. He got in and pulled the car door closed; the drivers turned on their red lights and raced down the street.

The demonstration had silenced the city. The avenues were strewn with boulders, and barbed wire lay in coils on every sidewalk. Recent graffiti alluded to the attack on the barracks, and army troops patrolled the avenues.

A few months ago, when the ambassador invited me over, I was flattered, Santiago thought. Now I'm afraid. Who will be there? What will be decided? When the car pulled up to the gate, he was cracking his knuckles. At the entrance stood a doorman dressed in black, holding an umbrella and carrying a rifle over his shoulder. Mario's Mercedes was parked nearby. The front door opened noiselessly and revealed Carl Crystal.

"Good evening," he said. His voice was cold. He didn't extend his hand. "This way, please."

They crossed the large vestibule and went into the reception room. It was full of familiar faces. Santiago knew he had been the last to arrive and felt suddenly self-conscious about his casual clothes. Ambassador Hamilton, seated in the pink chair near the fireplace, stood to shake his hand.

"We just got settled," Hamilton said, gesturing to the rest of the party. "I guess we're all old friends, aren't we?" A slight smile crossed his lips.

Santiago turned to face the other guests. Caridad was sitting on a sofa next to Mario. Beside them sat General Roca, nodding and frowning. And to the general's left, looking blank, sat Antonio Fernández. Santiago approached his father-in-law; Fernández nodded and said nothing.

A tuxedoed waiter handed Santiago a scotch and soda. Hamilton said to Crystal, "I think everyone's been served now. Please tell the waiters they may go."

Crystal and the waiters left. The room fell silent. Santiago brought his drink to his lips and fixed his eyes on the fire.

"Well," Ambassador Hamilton said. "I'm glad to see you all made it here safe and sound. What a day."

Santiago lit a cigarette with trembling hands. Holding his breath, he counted to ten and took a long sip of scotch.

Hamilton turned to Santiago. "It was necessary to have this meeting tonight because we can't waste a minute," he said, emphasizing every word, staring at Santiago.

"Your excellency is referring to . . . ?" said Santiago.

"The escape of Gonzalo Santos." Hamilton gave Santiago an imperious nod.

"The real problem is your insolence." It was General Roca.

Santiago looked at the general, whose eyes were stony and dark. He remained silent, aware that in Colombia a civilian must never contradict, much less slight, a military man.

"Treason is treason," added Fernández.

Santiago looked at Caridad, who looked away.

General Roca cleared his throat. "This state of affairs cannot continue, Dr. Villalba," he said. "We will not allow you to lead this country into chaos."

Santiago shook his head and wondered if the point of this meeting was to pick on him.

Mario broke in. "When I recommended you to my father for the ministry, I never thought we would be confronted with this kind of shit." He was turning scarlet with anger. "It's thanks to you that we had a massacre of five thousand. Don't you realize the position you've put us in?"

Best to play along, Santiago decided. "I'll resign here and now," he said. No one seemed satisfied.

"What's the matter with you, you traitor?" shouted Mario. "You're a fucking terrorist. We ought to hang you by your balls."

"Dr. Villalba," said General Roca sternly. "What we want is for you to sign a confession of guilt, and to admit your mistakes in a public trial. If you don't—"

His speech was interrupted.

Carl Crystal and a guard, their hands and feet tied, fell through the door and onto the rug. Four people dressed in army fatigues with stockings over their heads burst into the room and pointed pistols at the group.

"Hands up!" one of them shouted.

Santiago felt not fear but relief. One of the terrorists pulled the stocking off her head. He recognized Policarpa Samper, the woman whose announcements had broken into the evening news. She leveled a heavy revolver at General Roca. Wearing army fatigues that were much too large, she might, in other circumstances, have looked like a clown.

The ambassador stood up as if to receive his new guests. "Let's be reasonable," he said. "Surely there's no need—"

"Shut up," Policarpa growled. "Everyone on their feet. Right now."

The small group rose from their seats. General Roca, the last one to obey, said in an officious tone, "I advise you to surrender. Subversion is not an alternative. If you give up peacefully, I promise you a civilian trial."

Policarpa laughed, rose on her toes like a ballerina, and spat in the general's face. He slapped her. She lost her balance and fell backward against Fernández.

"Pig!" shouted one of the terrorists. He flung himself at the general.

"Get back," ordered Policarpa. Composing herself, she fired a clean shot between the general's eyes. His legs folded, and he fell back into a chair. Blood oozed from the wound; his open eyes seemed to express surprise.

Fernández was whimpering. "No more violence," he pleaded.

Putting the muzzle of her gun to his face, Policarpa said, "You bloodsucking vampire." She slammed the butt of the gun against his nose. The cartilage snapped audibly. Fernández fell to his knees, put his hands to his nose, and made wet, sputtering sounds.

"Everybody on the floor, except the *gringo* and the tyrant's son," Policarpa said.

Santiago, Caridad, and Antonio lay down on the rug. One of the terrorists tied their hands behind their backs, bound their legs together, and ordered Mario to take off his pants. Mario stood still. Policarpa cocked her pistol. "Do you want me to take them off for you?" she asked.

Mario's hands were shaking; the trousers tangled around his feet. Two of the terrorists leaned over him, inspected his legs as if they were archaeological wonders, and exchanged puzzled looks. "Which is the wooden leg?" asked one. The other kicked Mario in the right shin. Mario cried out in pain. The men hauled him onto the sofa and began to pull on his left leg.

"No, no, please, no," he pleaded.

"Silence!" Policarpa shouted.

She approached Mario and aimed the gun at his temple. "If you don't take the leg off *right now* you can kiss the world goodbye, cocksucker."

Mario unfastened his leg. Policarpa took it by the shoe and exclaimed, "It's heavy as hell." One of her henchmen tied Mario by the hands and leg to the sofa. Then the terrorists gathered around Ambassador Hamilton.

"You're coming with us, sweetie," Policarpa said. The ambassador frowned like a child about to burst into tears.

Policarpa took Mario's leg and raised it above her head. "This leg, paid for with the lives of comrades fallen in the struggle, is a symbol of the oppression in our country," she declared. "This symbol of imperialism and torture will be returned to its owner only when the Colombian people are free."

The terrorists exited, prodding the ambassador before them. Santiago wondered, almost longingly, why they had not taken him hostage as well.

14 ▽

Santiago was dropped off at his apartment before daybreak. He sat in the dark living room and rubbed his wrists, still raw from the ropes. His predicament seemed inescapable. To whom would he finally fall victim: the government or the terrorists? He drank some cognac and snorted some cocaine; neither soothed him. He took his glass and went out to the terrace.

The air was cold and still; dawn had not yet broken through the curtain of night. The lights of the city were strings of dots that extended for miles, broken in places by the poorer neighborhoods. Blanca wasn't lying about the electricity, he thought. His eyes wandered over the landscape as the events of the past few days reeled through his mind. Suddenly, there was a violent shaking; the glass of cognac leaped out of his hand and broke on the mosaic-tiled floor. He looked around. The terrace flower pots seemed to have gone into convulsions, and the crystal chandeliers inside the penthouse were swinging wildly. An angry roar erupted, apparently from the bowels of the earth. He closed his eyes and concentrated on breathing regularly and keeping his balance. A minute later, he dared hope the tremor was over.

He turned to walk into the living room and found that his legs were weak. Bracing himself against the wall, he walked, step by deliberate step, to the living-room sofa and dropped into it. Would the shaking return? Adrenaline surged through him; relieved, he jumped to his feet and ran through the kitchen to Blanca's room.

It was too dark to see. "Blanca, are you there?" he called. There was no answer. With his hands he found and patted the bed. It was made; no one had slept in it that night.

He walked into the living room, wondering if Blanca had escaped the massacre. Could she be staying with her parents? Perspiring yet chilly, he plucked at his shirt. He sat down and snorted the remaining cocaine. The drug clarified his fears. Now he understood: Blanca was a terrorist. Her eyes were as hard as Policarpa Samper's.

Convinced that Policarpa was on the way there, he ran to his bedroom, locked the door, turned out the lights, and lit a candle. The room smelled strange. When he was a child and fear overcame him, he had hidden in bed. He longed for that sense of security now. He moved quietly to the side of the bed, sat down on the edge to take off his shoes, then leaped up. Something seemed to have bitten him. He took a deep breath and reminded himself that he must not let paranoia get out of control. He put his hands on the bed. Something like a bulky, heavy bundle was indeed in it. Tentatively, delicately, he pulled the bedspread back, and found himself looking at the bald head and violet face of his father's corpse. Santiago's breath stuck in his throat and his nose started to run. He yanked the covers back and dropped them on the floor. Before him lay his father's embalmed body.

He closed his eyes and hoped he was hallucinating, but when he opened them the corpse was still there. It's real, he thought. And it's come back to get me.

Santiago felt a momentary desire to run from the apartment, but a perverse fascination kept him in the room and made him study his father's body. It was smaller now; the black suit it wore was much too big. The greenish face had shrunk to the size of a cantaloupe, and its wrinkles were more pronounced than Santiago remembered. In the candlelight, its features seemed frozen by fear.

Santiago paced around the bed. How could he get rid of the body? He could set the entire apartment on fire. But bones don't burn, and if the firemen arrived promptly—however remote that possibility was in Bogotá—someone might be able to identify the remains. He pulled the curtains open. Dawn was already bleaching out the black of the sky.

A sharp carving knife, he decided, was what he needed. He went into the kitchen and looked through the drawers. In the pantry, he found a machete and two large black plastic bags.

He swung his bedroom door open and flipped on the overhead light. Under it, the corpse looked even more macabre than it had by candlelight. A wave of nausea passed through Santiago; he went back into the corridor, leaned against the wall, and breathed deeply. It must be the smell of the chemicals used to preserve the body, he thought.

As nausea left him another feeling took its place: not terror or fear but anger. Anger at the net of intrigue, corruption, and rot his father had left him; and above all anger at the man's persistence. Like a cyst that hurts, doesn't respond to treatment and doesn't have the grace to go away on its own, Santiago thought. He had planned just to dismember the corpse; now he wanted to punish it, and to banish it for good, no matter what the cost.

Santiago returned to his room, raised the machete, and brought it down on the corpse's neck. The head rolled as if looking to the side, and a bluish liquid seeped from the yawning wound. The blow had severed the head completely from the body. The chemical smell— formaldehyde, Santiago guessed—rose with renewed force. Dizziness and nausea again gripped Santiago. Determined not to be overpowered, he hacked at the body, struggling to regain his equilibrium.

The queasiness passed. He stood back. The strokes had accomplished little more than opening a number of large, wet blue wounds. The job would have to be done more methodically. He knelt by the corpse's side and, with the help of the machete, removed its clothes. The body beneath was as cold as an Andean dawn. He raised the stiff arms and sawed at the shoulders and elbows. The arteries were like resistant cord; the muscles were hard; the bones were as brittle as chicken wings.

As he worked, he put the limbs and pieces in the garbage bags. When he was finished with the body, he removed the bedding and stuffed it too into the bags. He went through the living room, opened the apartment door, and peered out; no one was in the hall. The first bag was heavy and almost too full; he was sweating, grunting, and pushing it with his body before it finally disappeared down the incinerator's narrow chute. The other bag vanished more easily.

Santiago returned to the apartment and poured himself a large drink. The cadaver was finally, irretrievably, gone. He raised the glass in a toast. *"Papá,"* he said. "May you burn in hell."

A dried eucalyptus branch stood in a vase by the bar. Santiago pulled it out, took it into the bedroom, and lit it, hoping the aromatic smoke would disguise the smell of formaldehyde. He opened the windows, threw the branch out, and felt the fresh morning breeze. Night was over, and behind Monserrate the sun was rising like a luminous wafer.

He took out clean sheets and made the bed. Then he stood under the shower for a long time. While shaving, he paused; his eyes in the mirror looked feverish. He turned the radio to chamber music. It was seven A.M.

Breakfast was on the table and the kitchen radio was tuned to a salsa station. Blanca had survived. When had she come in? Or had she been hiding the whole time, spying on him? He looked at the cup he held; he'd unconsciously drunk half of the coffee. He put it down and looked through the newspapers for stories about the embassy break-in. Every paper covered General Roca's assassination, but none mentioned the abduction of Hamilton or of Mario's wooden leg. Santiago switched on the television news; the announcer had no further details.

The kitchen door opened and Blanca came into the room. Santiago indulged his fear, wondering whether the girl knew about what had happened during the night.

"How are you this morning, Don Santiago?" she said.

He stared at the television and didn't answer. Just as Blanca stood by his side and looked at the screen, the image blurred and in the announcer's place appeared the flag of F-69. Policarpa Samper stepped in front of it.

"Fellow Colombians," she began. "F-69 has dealt another blow to the Colombian oligarchy and to international imperialism. Last night, in the name of the Colombian people, we freed our country of the torturer General Roca. We kidnapped the gangster ambassador of Uncle Sam, and also took as hostage the leg of the depraved murderer Mario Simán."

The camera cut back to show Mario's artificial leg.

Policarpa's voice continued: "This leg is a symbol of our people's oppression. It will be returned to its owner only when Colombia is free."

Visible again, Policarpa pulled a snapshot of Stuart G. Hamilton from the pocket of her olive-green jacket. In the photo, the ambassador was on knees and naked; a pathetic expression was in his eyes.

Blanca snickered, then caught herself. "Things are bad," she said. "Real bad."

Policarpa spoke again. "Stuart G. Hamilton is a notorious CIA agent. F-69 has taken him hostage until all political prisoners are released." She paused, then, raising her voice, added, "And until the Panama Canal, stolen by the imperialist Theodore Roosevelt, is returned to Colombia. Long live the comrades fallen in battle!" The young woman's voice was quivering with determination. "Long live all liberation movements! Long live F-69 and the Colombian people!"

The screen went blank. Santiago got up, turned off the set, and went into his bedroom; before he closed the door, Blanca had turned the television back on and had taken his place on the sofa.

He threw himself on the bed and buried his face in the pillows. The chemical smell of the corpse, still strong in the mattress, clawed at his stomach. He ran to the bathroom and vomited a pale greenish liquid. He retched until only a gluey, foul-smelling slime coated his lips and tongue. He washed his face, rinsed his mouth, and lay down with a lotion-soaked cloth over his nose. The telephone rang.

"Santiago?" It was Caridad. "Listen, I can't talk, especially on the phone, but I advise you to leave Colombia, today."

Santiago sat up. "Why?"

"What do you mean, *why*? You're a known subversive, that's why. If the army doesn't get you, Mario will. Either way it's trouble, and I wouldn't want to be in your shoes." Caridad's voice was hushed. "If I were you, I'd find out what flights leave the country this afternoon. You'd better start packing; you don't have much time." She paused. "Santiago, before you leave Colombia there's something I want you to know. I love you. I want to come with you."

Santiago's head spun. "Caridad . . ." he began.

"I can't talk anymore. Do you have a valid passport?"

"Yes, I think so. I have to check."

"Pack your bags and try to get seats on a flight leaving early this afternoon. I'll pick you up in an hour. *Ciao.*"

Santiago sat for a minute with the receiver in his hands. Could he have heard right? He pulled himself together and looked for his passport. It was still valid, thank God. He found a suitcase in his closet and filled it with essentials: a bathrobe, a pair of pajamas, a toothbrush, a razor, a few shirts, underwear, and photographs of his mother, stepsister, and wife, and the two *tunjos*. Then he remembered that the *tunjos* had been given to him by Mario. He replaced them on the bookcase.

His largest bank account was in Paris. He made reservations for two on the KLM flight for France that afternoon. In the living room, the television was still on, but Blanca was gone. She'll be in charge now, he thought dryly. He sat down, lit a cigarette, and caught his breath. Cocaine—that's what I need now, he decided. He got up to look for some.

Two hours later Caridad arrived. Wearing ropes of gold jewelry, leather pants, leopard boots, and an ermine coat, and with rings covering most of the flesh of her fingers, she looked like a savage queen.

On the terrace, they hid from the sun under an umbrella. Caridad took his hand and talked to him in a low voice. She told him she had been the mistress of General Roca, who had seduced her when she was a teenager; and that she loathed her job at PAX, but that Roca had insisted she take it and keep it. Now she was free. "I've never known a man so respectful of a woman's feelings," she said. "I want to be your wife. I want to go far, far away with you and start over with a clean slate."

Suspicion and doubt nagged at Santiago. He looked in Caridad's eyes; they seemed soft and sincere. She kissed his lips.

Caridad got up. "Cardinal Hoyos is at the cathedral waiting for our call," she said. Santiago nodded, and Caridad walked to the telephone. Santiago went in the bedroom, found the rings from his marriage to Beatrice, and put them in his pocket. Caridad, a smile on her lips, was waiting for him by the front door.

They drove across Bogotá to the cathedral. The city looked as if it had been ransacked. Store windows were broken, and smoke was still rising from some charred buildings. The military and police were out in force; today they seemed to be favoring submachine guns, bazookas, and rocket launchers. But a good portion of the city's population, apparently unconcerned, was making its rounds through the wreckage and weaponry. The daily routine had begun again; traffic was heavy.

Caridad lifted the cathedral's brass knocker, shaped like a closed fist, and let it fall three times. A choirboy opened the gate. Cardinal Hoyos, in full ecclesiastical robes, stood before the main altar. Beside him stood two of Caridad's employees.

"What the hell?" said Santiago. He hadn't yet conquered all his suspicions.

Caridad shushed him. "They're the witnesses," she whispered. The cardinal kissed Caridad on both cheeks and shook the groom's hand.

Santiago walked through the ritual like a zombie, staring at the unusual witnesses. He knew he was marrying Caridad because he didn't have the strength *not* to. She would quench his loneliness, he thought.·

When the ceremony was over, Cardinal Hoyos saw the newlyweds to the door. "Hurry," he urged. "Good luck and may God be with you." He made the sign of the cross.

Caridad remained quiet most of the way to the airport, smoking incessantly, and breaking the silence only to curse the heavy traffic. She parked in the area reserved for government officials. Santiago noticed that her only luggage was a lightweight shoulder bag, and that she abandoned her car without the slightest hesitation.

"I'll buy you another car as soon as possible," he said. He looked at Caridad and knew that what he felt for her —whether love or hate or desire or revulsion—was both bewildering and thrilling. Her lips curled in an enigmatic smile.

Inside the airport, policemen and soldiers were checking the documents of what seemed to be thousands of people. Small children carried absurd toys and pets; women waving passports cried and embraced; men flashed rolls of bills in the faces of airline employees.

Caridad took Santiago firmly by the arm. "It's okay," she said. "Everything will be all right." She guided them through the mob. "It's always like this when the going gets rough. Everyone tries to get out."

When they reached the KLM desk, Caridad flashed her official ID at one of the attendants. A few minutes later, the loudspeakers announced that the flight was boarding. They climbed the steps of the broken escalator to the lounge.

The din in the waiting room was even louder than it had been downstairs. The employee who stamped their passports apologized for the turbulence of the crowd. When they were asked to pay the exit tax, Santiago discovered that in his haste to leave the penthouse, he had forgotten to take any cash; Caridad gave him a frown of annoyance and dug into her purse.

Hand in hand, the couple dashed down the corridor to the departure gates, ran down the stairs, and reached the open air of the KLM boarding area. They were the last passengers in line.

Santiago mopped his forehead with his handkerchief and tried to calm himself. Caridad kissed the lobe of his ear. "Now you're mine," she breathed.

As they approached the stairs that led into the belly of the plane, Santiago spotted the wedding witnesses standing near a stewardess. A chill came over him. Maybe they've come to see her off, he thought. Suddenly from behind them stepped Francisco Gutiérrez.

Santiago grabbed Caridad's wrist. "What's that guy doing here?" he said.

Caridad shook herself loose, took a small pistol out of her bag, and pointed it at Santiago. She waved to her flunkies. "Take him away," she ordered. Her face twisted into a sneer.

Santiago felt himself go cold and rigid. He seemed to be lost in his worst fears. "Caridad, don't do this," he begged, as the thugs bent his arms behind him. "Why? Why?"

The coldness in her eyes spread across her face. "Get him out of here," she shouted.

Santiago screamed, "They're going to kill me! They're going to kill me!" Gutiérrez led the thugs, who dragged Santiago behind a maintenance truck.

Caridad put her revolver in her purse, stood in front of Santiago, and, with the long black fingernails Santiago had found so fascinating, scratched his face. "Traitor," she snarled. "Did you think I was going to run off with you? Really, Santiago." Twenty yards behind her, ground-crew members tending the KLM flight were wagging directional signals.

Santiago shook his head, hoping to awaken, and instead felt blood fly from his face.

"Stupid idiot," she crowed. "Don't you get it? I'm your wife now! When you die, your entire fortune will belong to me." She turned to her men. "Do it," she said.

"Caridad, please . . ." Blood clouded Santiago's vision.

"Just a minute." Caridad drew very close. "Before you go where you belong, there's one thing I'd like you to know. I killed Beatrice so that I could marry you. And after her death, I made an alliance with that asshole Antonio Fernández." The jet's engines, warming up, drowned the sound of her laugh.

Anger overcame him. Santiago kicked backward, caught one of the thugs in the shin, twisted loose, and threw himself at Caridad. She dodged, bumped against a passing stewardess, and fell on her back. Santiago leaped on her and pressed his thumbs on her throat. Gutiérrez took hold of his shoulder, then fell away, clutching at his bloody chest. Santiago looked up. The woman in the stewardess's uniform was Policarpa Samper. In a military squat, both hands on an automatic pistol, she wheeled, fired a burst of shots into Caridad's gorillas, and turned toward Santiago. "Murderer, murderer!" she screamed in a banshee voice, and squeezed the trigger. Caridad's head burst like a ripe pomegranate. Her mouth flew open and her long, pink tongue curled. She died with Santiago's fingers still digging into her flesh.

Policarpa pointed the pistol at Santiago and shouted, "Get up!"

A shot sounded from somewhere to the side and something punctured Santiago's upper arm. The impact threw him onto the macadam.

"Get up," Policarpa yelled. "You're not that badly hurt." She turned to the plane and hollered, "Gonzalo, where are you?"

Santiago pulled himself to his feet. From a distant departure gate policemen and soldiers were running toward him; some were already kneeling and firing. He ran in a crouch toward the plane. Gonzalo Santos, dressed as a mechanic, stood behind the movable staircase. Santiago joined him. Above, the plane's door swung open, and terrorists emerged.

As they opened fire, one of them shouted, "They're killing Policarpa!"

Santiago looked behind. The young woman, her feet planted far apart, was firing stoically toward the advanced uniformed men. Her back was a sprinkler gushing blood.

"I have a bomb!" Policarpa threatened. An explosion rocked the earth and Santiago saw Policarpa burst into dozens of pieces; flames chased her head into space. Black smoke enveloped the area.

"Come on. Let's go!" said Gonzalo. He pushed Santiago up the stairs.

His right arm limp, Santiago stumbled, picked himself up, and scrambled to the door. An armed man reached out, pulled him all the way through, and swung the door shut. "Gonzalo," Santiago said.

"He wants to stay," said the man. "Now get out of the way."

The plane began to taxi as Santiago pushed his way past fearful faces down the main aisle. The last two seats were unoccupied; he sat by the window. In the front of the passenger compartment, a masked man was shouting orders.

The plane wheeled onto the main runway and gained speed. Holding the wounded arm, Santiago leaned his head on the headrest and gazed out the window. He wasn't sure, but he thought he could make out the maintenance truck in flames. He closed his eyes. When the plane rose from the ground a slight dizziness took hold of him; he bunched up a handkerchief and pressed it against the wound. He turned to the window. Already the view was like a lushly illustrated map. The savannah glowed emerald. Santiago bid farewell to the golden land of iridescent hummingbirds and double rainbows and infinite orchids.

The bleeding had slowed and he'd begun to doze when a timid female voice roused him. It seemed to be calling from a great distance.

He opened his eyes; Blanca stood before him holding a cumbersome package. "This is for you," she said, handing it to him and sitting down in the empty seat beside him.

Santiago wiped his hands on his pants, then tore away the wrapping. Inside were Mario Simán's artificial leg and what looked like the sword of Simón Bolívar. He gave the girl an uncomprehending look.

She leaned back and looked at him, an exalted gleam in her eye. "Santiago," she said, "now it's up to us."

Madrid 1976
New York 1982